To Chloe, with thanks

1

Ned had been given choices. The trouble was he didn't like any of them. He could stay at school like other sad boys who had nowhere to go for the holidays. He could go to his cousin who was four years older and treated him like a slave. Or he could spend the two weeks with his Great-Aunt Ellen, who had a cat but no television and cooked him huge meals three times a day. It had to be Aunt Ellen, the best option in a bad scene.

So now he sat opposite his geography teacher, 'Grrh' Upchurch, who was escorting him to London. From there he'd be put on another train heading east, in the direction of the small seaside town where his great-aunt lived.

'Your mother's not too well then?'

Ned saw Grrh (named by the boys for his bad temper) was trying to be kind. Grrh put down his newspaper on the table between them and his stiff red face contorted in an effort to display concern.

'She's going to have a baby, sir, and the doctors told her not to travel till it arrives. She's in Australia.'

'And your father's stayed with her?'

'Yes, sir.' There seemed nothing to add to this. In his heart of hearts he thought it odd that his dad should put his mum and a so far non-existent baby above a definitely living son, but grown-ups had strange priorities.

'They'll come for me as soon as they can,' he added, so as not to seem too pathetic.

'Parents tend to collect their sons eventually,' agreed Grrh.

It was midday by the time they arrived in London. Ned had already eaten his sandwiches – stale bread and curling ham. They'd have turned into planks if he'd kept them any longer.

He knew the station because it was where his parents usually met him, standing in a noisy crowd of other children and parents. Today there was just him and Grrh. He'd left school a day later than everybody else while arrangements were made with his great-aunt.

He'd stayed with her once before when there'd been another kind of emergency – that was the thing about having a mother and father who travelled for their work. They had a tendency to get stuck out of England. He wouldn't even be in boarding school otherwise.

'Want a drink, while we wait, do you?'

They went together to a noisy bar with lots of mirrors, where Ned was surprised by a dwarf with huge blue eyes and tufty blond hair coming towards him. He was even more surprised when he realised it was him. Would he never grow?

'What'll it be? Coke or juice? Or something stronger to celebrate the end of term?' Grrh cackled.

Ned had often noticed grown-ups had a particularly silly sense of humour where children were concerned.

'Coke, sir.'

It was no fun watching Grrh's face turning a deeper shade of red as he knocked back a couple of beers and something stronger in a small glass. Ned was glad when it was time for his train.

'There you are, boy.' Grrh handed him his bag. 'Now the world's your oyster. Capital of East Anglia, what?'

Ignoring this further attempt at a joke, Ned thanked the teacher politely and hopped on the train, dragging the bag behind him.

The train wasn't full and he easily found a seat by the window. He got out the packet of Fruitellas he'd saved for just this moment, placed his book on his lap, and settled down for the journey.

It was outside Colchester that he noticed the train was going remarkably slowly. He shielded his eyes against the afternoon sun and saw that the rows of cherry trees in the fields along the track were passing at hardly more than walking pace.

'Now what's wrong?' said a cross woman across the aisle to no one in particular.

Ned was worried too. A taxi was coming to meet him at the station. He just hoped it waited for him. He knew it was a good three-quarter of an hour's drive to Great-Aunt Ellen's cottage on the coast.

He got out his discman and headphones, but his heart wasn't in *Three Doors Dawn*. His parents had promised him a mobile phone for months now but nothing had turned up. It was 'out of sight, out of mind' with those two.

The train was absolutely stationary now.

'So what's going on?' shouted the same angry woman at the harassed guard trying to hurry through the carriage.

'Technical difficulties, madam.' He shot away.

Three hours later and hooked up to a fresh engine, Ned's train finally crawled into his station. For the hundredth time, he looked at his watch. Nearly two hours late. No hope that the taxi would hang around that long.

Sure enough, by the time he'd dragged his bag round to the station's entrance, there was not a car in sight. Not a person either.

He felt self-conscious standing there all on his own with the sun beginning to go down. He looked at his watch yet again. It was nearly six. He suddenly felt very shy and young. He never could understand the way he felt all right inside – not actually fearful anyway – but outside, his body got all nervous, even shaking sometimes. Now he needed to approach a stranger and tell him his problem.

But who to ask? The station was still deserted, the

ticket office closed. He looked around anxiously. At that moment he heard a car approaching. It swirled up to where he stood and stopped abruptly. A grey-stubbled face looked out of the window.

'Ned, is it? For Seaburgh?'

'Yes, yes. Th-that's me.' He was stuttering a little.

'Bob couldn't wait. Stick your bag in the back and hop in.'

The moment he got in the back – the front seat was piled high with magazines – they were off at the same wild speed the car had arrived.

'Got to be here again in not much over the hour,' explained the driver, lighting himself a cigarette. 'What you doing in a queer old place like Seaburgh? The place the world forgot, I call it.'

'I'm staying with my great-aunt.' He tried to avoid looking at the hedges and walls rushing by. He thought it was just his luck to travel in a train that made him anxious by going slow and a taxi that made him anxious by going fast.

'That figures. Seaburgh's the only place where you'd find a great-aunt these days. Called Gertrude, is she?'

'Ellen.'

'Great-Aunt Ellen. I wish you the best of it.' The driver laughed mockingly and put on his radio. Now he amused himself by attacking various sports commentators as obvious rubbish, dough-balls and ham-heads.

Despite their speed, it was just about dark by the time they approached Seaburgh. For some time, the landscape had become open and very flat, with the occasional church spire looming out of the dusk. Ned peered into the darkness and saw a few pale houses on either side of the road and then street lighting, golden beams in the gloom.

'Sniff the sea, can you?' The driver turned his attention once more to his passenger. He switched off the radio.

'Are we nearly there?'

'I was hoping *you'd* tell me that.'

'It's called Lilac Cottage.'

'Need a bit more, don't I?' said the driver impatiently. 'Where's your great-aunt put her Rose Cottage then?'

'Lilac Cottage. On the front, I think. I mean you can hear the sea . . .' Ned's voice petered out helplessly.

'That'll have to do then, won't it? The front. Not too bright, are you? I drive you there and you pick out the house spanking-quick. I told you, didn't I, I'd never have come if Bob wasn't owed a favour.'

Ned realised they'd reached the front when there was an absence in front of the headlights. Nothing. Nothing at all! Just the murky air, swirling mysteriously ahead. It was the ocean, miles and miles of it.

'Left or right?'

The road had come to an end. On each side was a row of cottages. Left or right? Ned had no idea.

'Just drop me here!' he cried impulsively. He was excited by the nearness of the sea and it seemed easier

6

to make his own way than to put up a moment longer with his driver.

'First one on the left then?'

'Yes. That's it,' lied Ned, and the moment the car stopped, he was out like a flash and pulling his bag after him.

'Cheers.'

Ned watched as the car sped away. There were a couple of lights along the front but he was still shocked by the total darkness and the silence. As he hesitated which way to turn, he suddenly heard a new sound: the quiet swish of waves on shingle. He listened more carefully. He remembered when he'd stayed with his aunt before, his bedroom had been at the front, and he'd gone to sleep with that same rhythmic sound.

Making up his mind, he turned right and, leaving his bag, started to walk purposefully along the row of cottages. Soon he recognised Lilac Cottage, a narrow house set back from the others.

At that moment, there was a shattering noise, at first distant, then coming very fast in his direction. He stepped back automatically as an ambulance, striped with yellow and green, its siren screaming, shot by him and screeched to a halt. Right opposite his aunt's house. He watched, unseen by anyone. One man opened the doors at the back of the ambulance, then went into the house with another man. A couple of minutes later, they were out again, carrying a stretcher.

Ned crept a little closer. On the stretcher lay his Great-Aunt Ellen, eyes closed, face as pale as a ghost. It was all happening so quickly that he had no time to think. In a matter of seconds, Aunt Ellen had disappeared inside the ambulance, the doors were closed, and the ambulance was away again. Just as noisily as before. He stood where he was, too surprised to move or even shout.

2

Ned stood still, trying to work things out, for quite a few minutes. Was his aunt dying? Or even dead? Gradually, the gently lapping waves soothed his nerves and he took heart. He also felt extremely hungry. He'd eaten nothing except Fruitellas since his sandwich that morning. First things first. He must get into the house.

He returned down the road to get his bag and then stood looking at Lilac Cottage. It was so small that it was almost unnoticeable. He could see all the windows were tightly shut and it hardly seemed worth trying the front door, although he did. It was locked. He stood back once again. To one side of the house, there was a wooden gate that he remembered led to a tiny garden with one twisted old lilac tree. Maybe his aunt had left a window open at the back?

It was easy enough to open the little gate and go in the garden. He was peering upwards when he nearly jumped out of his skin. Something was rubbing against his leg. A loud purring gave him the hint. He put his hand down and felt in the darkness a soft furriness.

'Oh, Sid, you're here!' Of course, it was his aunt's black cat, Sidonie – Sid for short – enormous and very friendly. But before Ned could crouch down and give her a good stroking, she'd sprung away again. Ned could just see her against the pale paint of the cottage.

'Now what?' he whispered to himself. He watched Sid pick her way delicately towards the building. She crouched back slightly and then leaped on to a windowsill. Without hesitating, she raised one paw and carefully edged it round the corner of the window. Ever so gently, she pulled the window open.

Ned decided Sid was the cleverest and most helpful cat in the world. As the cat's tail disappeared inside the cottage, he heaved his bag nearer the wall and prepared to get through the window too. His bag would make a very useful step.

For once he was glad to be small. Up close, the window was tiny, and at one moment his shoulders seemed firmly stuck so he couldn't move one way or the other. He was beginning to panic when he heard a mewing from below him. Clearly, Sid thought he should try harder. With an extra-strong push, nearly diving headfirst on to the floor, he was through.

'Cheers, Sid!' Ned swivelled round and jumped down. This time the cat did allow him to stroke her, but after a few seconds moved away. Ned followed her bushy tail, held high and straight like a sail.

He had landed in a little pantry, tacked on to the back of the house and leading into another bigger room. He felt for a light switch, then blinked dazedly.

After being in the dark so long, the light seemed extraordinarily brilliant.

When his eyes had calmed down he looked round and saw a table with two chairs and a wooden dresser, a small cooker and a fridge. The table was set with a meal for two: a loaf of bread, butter, ham, tomatoes, cheese, orange squash, and on the stove he could see a pan of baked beans ready to be heated. Great-Aunt Ellen must have prepared everything for their tea together and quite suddenly been taken ill.

He wouldn't think about that quite yet. His stomach was rumbling even louder than Sid was purring.

'OK, OK, give me a chance.' Sid was standing over an empty saucer on the floor. 'You must be the bossiest cat in the world.' Ned took a bottle of milk from the fridge and filled the saucer. Now he could get something for himself: a ham sandwich, followed by baked beans on toast.

Half an hour later, he was ready for action. Closely followed by Sid, he unlocked the back door and dragged in his bag. From then on, he did the following. The cat led him into every room – not that there were many. Downstairs, there was a front parlour – the old-fashioned word seemed suitable for the neat pretty room, with its chintzy sofa and chairs, its gold-framed mirror on the wall and rose-patterned rug. White lace curtains hung at the windows so that no one could look in, but through them Ned could sense the empty vastness of the sea. By the stairs that led from the

11

hallway there was a lavatory, and upstairs a bathroom and two small bedrooms: one back, one front.

Ned drew the curtains in the front room. This was where he would sleep. He noted a pile of old *Boy's Own* adventure stories, that he remembered from before, had been carefully piled on the bedside table.

Sid jumped on to the bed and arched her back invitingly. Ned bent to stroke her. 'Just right, isn't it? Don't know about you, Sid, but it makes me feel tired. How about I have a nice hot bath, then off to bed?'

Sid purred approvingly.

So Ned went downstairs, cleared the kitchen a bit – although washing up seemed a step too far – and returned up to the bathroom. He stood watching as hot water poured from the taps and enough steam swirled up to fill the room. Vaguely, he considered the idea that someone should be told he was here all on his own – apart from Sid, that is. But who should he tell? Definitely not Grrh – he didn't have his number anyway. Not his parents, who had worries enough. Anyway, they knew where he was. It was just that his aunt wasn't with him. He avoided picturing her grey face as she lay on the stretcher. The point was he was perfectly comfortable and perfectly safe.

Ned opened the window above his bed before he got into it. As he lay drifting, almost asleep, he could hear the waves again. They seemed louder than before, less soothing; but just as he was beginning to imagine rollers white-topped and crashing on the beach, the bed creaked and Sid landed with a heavy plop on his legs.

'Oh, Sid, you great lump! You might have broken my leg,' he grumbled.

By the time he'd settled the cat cosily by his hip, he was as near asleep as makes no difference and the waves had receded into their usual quiet pattern.

Later, a phone rang far away in the front parlour. Ned twitched a little in his sleep and then woke enough to be aware of Sid's warm bulk. By then the phone had stopped ringing.

'I like it here,' he mumbled into the darkness. 'In fact, there's no way I'm leaving. Get that, Sid.'

3

The morning was bright and breezy. Ned was woken by the flapping curtain. He knelt on his bed and looked out of his window. The grey and blue sea was crested with white lines of breaking waves. He'd been right the night before: the sea was rougher, although not with the wild rollers he'd imagined. It was April, and he remembered Great-Aunt Ellen telling him stories of giant spring tides. This was nothing to that.

Throwing on his clothes and deciding not to brush his teeth in celebration of the first day of the holidays, he jumped down the stairs and flung open the door to the kitchen. Sid was miaowing plaintively beside her empty plate.

'Oh, you old moaner!' Still, she was his only companion. He found a tin of cat food in the larder and noted that it was very well stocked with all kinds of food: fruit, vegetables, eggs, bread, various tins, cereal, biscuits, even a huge bag of toffees. His aunt had done enough shopping to last for days, if not weeks.

He took a handful of chocolate biscuits and turned

to feed Sid. He hadn't changed his mind from the night before. In fact, in the cheerful light of day, he felt even more convinced. He would stay exactly where he was until his parents came to collect him.

After breakfast, he put on his coat and filled the pockets with toffees. Time to do some exploring. He'd found a key to the front door on the mat, where the ambulance men must have posted it, so he was able to walk out like a free man and not some sort of intruder.

He did have a nervous moment when he saw the houses on either side, and wondered whether his aunt's departure had been noticed. Then he remembered she'd complained about a lack of neighbours because most of the houses in the row were holiday homes and only used in the summer. He looked more closely and saw that many of them were shuttered or had their curtains firmly drawn. Well, a lack of neighbours suited him perfectly – no one to interfere and tell him little boys can't live on their own!

He walked jauntily along the front. Occasionally, he gave a skip or ran for a few metres to show just how free he felt. At some distance behind him, Sid followed at a more dignified pace. She had the air of an old-fashioned nanny with a charge she didn't trust to behave himself.

After a while, Ned had passed the row of houses and found himself with only the pebbly beach, the sea and the sky. He was just deciding whether to go right down to the water when he spotted a group of tall black

15

wooden sheds and, beyond them, a fishing boat pulled up on the shore.

This looked more fun. He began to run. Behind him, Sidonie disdained to hurry and picked her way delicately over pebbles, shells, old ropes and general rubbish. Eventually, she stopped altogether and watched Ned, now and again swishing her tail a little as if anxious.

Ned had got on to the boat and managed to make his way to the front, which was not very easy as it was leaning at a severe angle. The wind blew his hair on end and made his trousers flap, and he imagined how it would be to be at sea with a force nine gale blowing. Fishermen would have faced that sort of thing on this very boat, although it was very battered now.

He investigated further and found there was no engine in the engine-room and no tiller at the back. Perhaps they were kept in one of those old sheds. He was beginning to feel cold and just slightly wishing there was a friend to share the day.

'Come over here, Sid!' he shouted to cheer himself up. 'Let's see what treasure we can find!'

But the door to the first wooden shed wouldn't open, nor the second, and he was just giving up on the third when he heard a scuffling sound from inside. He noticed that Sid, at his feet, had become rigid and her tail twitched fiercely at the tip.

'What is it? Rats? We can't get in, whatever it is. Anyway, I'm hungry. Let's go back.' He tried the door just once more. It didn't have a padlock and chain on it like the other sheds, and at one moment it seemed to give a little and then sharply jerked shut again, almost as if something was holding it from inside. A very big rat guarding his property, he thought, smiling at the idea before turning away.

Sid vanished somewhere as Ned walked back. The sea had come in quite a bit. He stood for a minute or two, watching the waves curl over and break on to the pebbles before sucking backwards and preparing for another surge forward. They were bringing with them seaweed and other bits and pieces. He remembered a term he'd read somewhere: 'flotsam and jetsam', the things brought in by the sea; some 'floating', some 'jetted' or thrown from a boat.

Curious, despite the chill wind that seemed to be getting right through his anorak, Ned started to crunch over the pebbles towards the sea.

He stopped again within half a metre of the pounding waves. Close to, they seemed much bigger; the weight of water, glassy and transparent as it was, came down with the force of a sledgehammer. He wouldn't like to have that lot on his head!

He tried to identify some of the little shards of shell and glass at the water's edge but, just as he bent down, a wave bigger than the rest rolled in so fast that he had to run backwards. Even so, he got his trainers wet.

He imagined his dad shouting at him, 'Ned, where're your *brains*!' It *was* stupid to start searching on the edge of a rough sea when the tide was coming in. He shivered a little. It was strange being so on his own. Even the sun had gone away. Definitely time for lunch.

Sid reappeared as Ned was frying up a packet of sausages – it seemed best to do the lot. Ned began to see why Sid was a huge size. 'You're such a greedy cat. I was planning to eat every single sausage myself, you know.' Obviously it made far more sense to eat a lot of one thing rather than a little from various different foods, all of which needed cooking. 'OK. Just one, then. Watch it doesn't burn your tongue.'

It was very silent inside the house as Ned and Sid ate their lunch – or at least it would have been, apart from the wind. The cottage was more solidly built than it looked but, even so, he could hear the wind straining in from the sea. He was holding his fifth sausage between his finger and thumb (why bother with cutlery that had to be washed?) when a loud crash startled him so much, he dropped the sausage on the floor. It was immediately gobbled up by Sid.

The noise was from *inside* the house. Upstairs, he thought. Heart thudding, he went out of the kitchen and through to the hall. He looked up the stairs. Immediately there was another crash. Stiffening his sinews, he took two stairs at a time and entered his bedroom just in time for a third crash.

'So that's what it is!' he exclaimed out loud with relief. He jumped on the bed and caught hold of the banging window. As he carefully hooked the latch – he couldn't have done it properly before – he looked out and saw the sky and sea were both the same thick grey colour, only lightened by white-crested waves rushing in, one after the other.

He'd been planning to go back to the beach. Now he wasn't so sure. Perhaps he'd see what the village had to offer. On the other hand, he didn't want to draw attention to himself. In a little place like this, a boy on his own was sure to be noticed. He could just imagine the nosy old ladies asking, 'Who does he belong to, then?' As if he belonged to anyone!

Feeling rather sorry for himself but trying not to admit it, he went back downstairs and into the front room. He didn't much like all the pink roses on the curtains and chairs, but he'd noticed some cupboards there. Maybe there was something interesting inside. Just his bad luck that his Great-Aunt Ellen was the only person left in England who didn't have a TV. Then he remembered where she was – in hospital, seriously ill, perhaps even dying – and felt guilty.

'Sorry, Aunt Ellen,' he said out loud, as if to the spirit of the house. But his words sounded odd in the weird little room. Talking to yourself was supposed to be the first sign of madness.

He bent down to one of the cupboards. At the same moment there was a harsh shrilling. Surely Aunt Ellen wouldn't have alarmed her cupboards! It took him a moment to realise it was a large, black, old-fashioned telephone ringing from a little table behind him.

Should he pick up the receiver? Would he be discovered? Sent away to somewhere horrible –

perhaps back to school? The phone rang and rang and eventually he couldn't bear it any more.

'Hello?'

'Hello. Can you hear me? Ned, is that you?'

'Oh, Dad! Yes it's me. I'm here.' To Ned's shame he suddenly felt like bursting into tears. It was just hearing his father's voice when he'd been alone so much.

'How are you? I called yesterday but you must have both gone to bed early. How's Aunt Ellen? Was your journey all right? What's the weather like? Have you been down to the sea yet?'

With so many questions, Ned had a moment to pick and choose his answers. But first he came up with a straightforward lie: 'Aunt Ellen's out at the moment,' which wouldn't have been such a lie if he hadn't added, 'she's gone shopping. For some ice-cream.'

'I knew she'd spoil you.' His dad sounded pleased. 'And you're settled in?'

'Oh, yes. Grrh – I mean Mr Upchurch brought me all the way.' The lying was coming more easily now. After all, he reminded himself, he was only trying to save them worrying. If they *were* worrying, of course. 'How's Mum?'

'Not too bad. No baby yet. But that's good news. The bigger it gets before it's born the better. You know we'll be back the moment Mum can travel. You do understand I can't leave her?'

'Of course, Dad.' Another lie. Why did he always come third-best?

'She sends you a hug.'

'Thanks, Dad.' Ned could hear his father was about to ring off and was suddenly overwhelmed by the sense he'd soon be alone again, maybe for days and days.

'What is it? Ned?'

Oh dear. He must have gulped or something tragic. 'I'm fine. It's fine here.'

'Good. Good. I'll say goodbye then.'

'Yes. I'm fine.'

After he'd put down the receiver, Ned sat for quite a while. Although it was only four o'clock, the sky seemed unnaturally dark and the wind was tearing round the little cottage as if determined to get in. Perhaps there was going to be a huge storm. Undecided whether to be excited or frightened, Ned turned on a lamp whose pink frilly shade cast a warm glow into the room, and returned to examining the cupboards.

4

The afternoon never grew any lighter. Ned took a flat, rectangular box he'd found in the cupboard and laid it on the kitchen table. It was large and black, with a picture of a castle on the front. The castle had six turrets and on each turret a different coloured flag flew: red, green, blue, yellow, orange, purple. Written in gold letters below it were the words: 'The Prince's Quest'. It all seemed very old-fashioned – he could imagine what some of his friends at school would make of it – but, if he wasn't going to go out (which he clearly wasn't), then he must have something to do.

Gingerly, he lifted off the lid. There was a name written on the inside: 'Mab Angel'. The handwriting was round and childlike.

Well, Mab Angel, he thought, as he took out the contents of the box. I hope you don't mind me playing your game, but I guess you don't have much choice.

And what a game it was! 'Wicked!' He unwrapped from tissue paper six perfectly modelled miniature knights. Each one had a different suit of armour and real feathers in his helmet: red, green, blue, yellow, orange or purple. He unfolded the board next and set them on it. The board was beautifully painted with a numbered path snaking through forests, over mountains, through marshes, over lakes and rivers, and even tunnelling into an underground region where strange rocks and potholes were home to snakes and other slimy animals. He got out more tissue-wrapped objects. The largest turned out to be a castle, like the one on the cover. He set it up carefully at the far side of the board. Around the foot of the castle was a rose-briar maze, the tangled and thorny branches painted in such a lifelike way that he hardly liked to put his finger on it.

The next package he opened was a princess-like creature dressed in real red velvet with a gold trim. Obviously, she belonged in the castle. Then there was a sorcerer, in a long purple robe patterned with silver stars and moons. Finally, he unwrapped a brilliant green dragon, with long scarlet tongue, white teeth and blazing red eyes.

As there was no rule book to help him, he decided to use three of the knights and, throwing the dice, race them through wood and wilderness towards the castle. He stationed the dragon, a fearsome guardian, just outside the castle's walls, and the wizard by a rocky desolate place.

He was so involved that he didn't notice an early night falling and the battering wind conjuring up sharp squalls of rain that flung themselves at the cottage as if they were the spears of an enemy.

It was only when Sid came shooting through the larder window and rubbed her thick damp fur against Ned's legs that he looked up. Luckily, the red knight had just won by reaching the castle, so he didn't mind stopping.

'Don't tell me, Sid. You're hungry. Me too.' He stroked the purring cat. 'Let's see what we can find. How about bacon and bacon?'

Although the kitchen was at the back of the cottage and the storm was coming in from the sea at the front, the wind was strong enough to rattle the jars on the larder shelves and blow a loose piece of paper to the floor. He went to the window through which he'd climbed in and closed it firmly.

'I'm battening down the hatches,' he told Sid as he returned to the kitchen (he hoped it wasn't a sign of madness to talk to a cat). 'The weather's getting really bad.'

The best plan was to eat supper and then head for bed and one of those *Boy's Own* books. By the time he'd got upstairs, followed at a short distance by Sid, the wind was howling round the cottage's roof and windows. Even in bed with the old-fashioned sheets, blankets and eiderdown pulled up to his ears, he couldn't help listening to the unearthly noise.

He couldn't read in this and certainly not sleep. He crouched up and opened the curtains to the window. He wanted to see what the ocean was up to but it was far too dark. He tried not to imagine that the waves sounded much closer than they had the night before.

There was no point in frightening himself. Storms came and storms went. This cottage had probably seen hundreds of storms worse than this one. All the same, when he lay down again, he found his heart was thudding in an uncomfortable way.

'Come on, Sid.' He made up his mind. 'We're moving.'

Great-Aunt Ellen's room was at the back of the house over the kitchen and was sure to be more peaceful.

Nevertheless, it felt strange to turn the handle of her door. He reminded himself that she was a very kind-hearted old lady and wouldn't want him to have a sleepless night.

It was immediately quieter, the noises of the storm muffled by the two doors. He got into bed, shivering a little at the coolness of the sheets.

'Come on, Sid. I need a hot-water bottle.' With the cat half on top of him he at last managed to sleep, the roar of the wind merging with his own breath and the cat's snoring.

Several hours passed, during which the winds and rain lashed themselves to a climax of frenzied onslaught. Ned, who had at first lain calmly, began to twitch and mutter. After a while Sid jumped off the bed and, after giving herself a good stretch, jumped up on the windowsill where she settled down again, hidden behind the curtain.

Ned turned restlessly. He was in the middle of a

dream about swimming in an underground lake, lit only by flaring torches attached to the wet and gleaming walls. Ahead of him, the black waters rippled and broke open and a vast creature with two protuberant eyes rose to its surface.

He managed to stifle a scream as he sat up abruptly. The underground scene vanished slowly and he returned to the reality of the storm. The darkness was very deep. He put out his hand to reach for Sid but found nothing. Probably her leaving had woken him, he told himself.

He lay back again and tried to compose himself but the wind was making even more aggressive noises than before, whistling at the windows, rattling at the door knobs. He could even hear the front door downstairs, pushing and straining.

Suddenly he heard something altogether different. The sweat of fear prickled at his scalp and he actually felt his hair lifting up from the roots. Above all the noises of the storm, he could hear footsteps. Someone was inside the house; someone was walking softly but audibly over his head.

5

Ned knew he wasn't very brave, not like some of his friends at school who were happy to jump off a roof or ride bicycles over level crossings without looking first. He had told himself they were stupid show-offs.

But as he lay in bed, shivering with a mixture of fear and cold, and all the time listening to those footsteps, he wished he'd got more guts. It was being utterly alone that made it worse, not even anyone to show off to.

He listened more carefully. The steps were light, not a grown man's, he thought hopefully. Of course, it must be Sid, gone up to the loft to look for mice.

'Sid! Sid!' he called joyfully, just to be sure.

Sid plopped off the windowsill and, not bothering to come to him, passed on to the door where she stood waiting.

He reached out to the switch of the bedside lamp. It cast a very small amount of light, highlighting the shadows more than anything. He lay quivering, too afraid to open the door. Sometimes the soft steps were overwhelmed by the noises of the storm but he was aware of them all the same, as if someone was walking in a circle.

'Miaow!' Sid complained at the door.

Making up his mind, Ned leaped out of bed, bounded across the room and flung open the door. Immediately the violence of the wind rose alarmingly. As Sid whisked out and disappeared, he stood uncertainly.

Should he return to his great-aunt's bedroom and listen all night to those horrid footsteps? Or was it better to return to his own bed and bury his head in the bedclothes?

He knew he wasn't thinking very clearly. People didn't walk round and round lofts in the middle of the night. But his head felt out of control, filled with horrible imaginings.

Yes! He would be better in his own bed. He turned the handle and opened the second door.

'Auff!' He was swept backwards by a strong wind that nearly blew him out of the room again.

'Shut the door. Quick! And I'll shut the window.'

Ned shut the door obediently and only then realised he was obeying not just a voice in his head, but a real voice, a soft girl's voice that had spoken out loud. Someone else was in the room.

He stayed by the door, listening acutely. The window was shut. He clearly heard the latch click. Whoever it was – it was far too dark to see – was crouching on the bed just as he had.

He approached warily. 'Who are you?'

'I'm Mab Angel. Gosh, you took a long time to wake up. I thought I'd have to play hopscotch and drop the pebble on your head.' Her voice was lighthearted and playful, the least threatening in the world.

'How did you get in?'

'Oh, I always come on wild nights.'

This didn't exactly answer Ned's question but he let it pass. He took several steps closer. 'Why are you here?'

'I thought you'd like someone to play with.' She sounded airily certain she was right. 'I used to live here, you know.'

'Did you?' Ned didn't know what was going on, but guessed she must be about his age – and it was extremely nice to be talking to a human being again.

'You must be freezing. Come on, you can sit in the other end of the bed.'

'It's a serious storm.' Ned advanced further. 'I thought I'd be blown right out of bed.'

'Yes. I used to think that. I used to make Ellen let me into her bed.'

'You know my Great-Aunt Ellen then?'

'Oh, yes. Very well.'

Somehow her knowing his aunt made it all seem a little less odd. Really, he couldn't see any reason why he couldn't accept her invitation to get into bed. His bare feet were freezing.

So, in a moment, Mab Angel and Ned were sitting opposite each other in the bed.

'Shall I put the light on?' asked Ned.

'It's more fun in the dark.'

She was right: it was fun and cosy. Even the storm seemed less all-enveloping now.

'I was worried before that the sea might come right up to the house.'

Mab Angel laughed gaily. 'I'm not frightened of the sea. It's done its worst with me.'

'What do you mean?'

'Nothing. It's all in the past now.' She paused and then said, as if to change the subject, 'Did you enjoy playing my game?'

'Your game? You mean Prince's Quest. The knights with feather plumes. Of course. Your name was written on the box.'

'My favourite game of all. When I stayed here, we played it every night.'

'I thought it was old. Like an antique.'

'It can't have been such fun playing against yourself. Maybe next time I come, we'll have a game.'

'Oh, yes!' agreed Ned, before wondering again about the oddity of the situation. He was more awake now and ready to ask questions. 'You said you only come on wild nights?'

'Usually that's when I'm wanted. To keep Ellen company. But now she's away, I'll visit you instead.'

'It might not be a wild night tomorrow,' persisted Ned. 'And why do you come at night anyway?'

'People are lonelier at night. They have bad dreams.'

'You can't just come out of nowhere. Where do you live?'

This time she cut him off firmly. 'Would you like me to tell you a story?'

'What sort of story?'

'You'll have to judge for yourself.'

'My mum used to tell me stories. On dark nights, when I was little, she'd sit on my bed and tell me stories till I went to sleep.'

'What sort of stories?'

'Adventure stories, about witches and ogres and ghouls . . .'

'Ghosts, you mean. Mine's a true story. Are you ready? Shut your eyes. It's easier to listen with your eyes shut.'

'I'm ready,' said Ned and, just as if he was a young child again, he settled down to listen to Mab Angel's soft, pretty voice.

6

'Once upon a time, a war was being fought throughout the world,' began Mab.

'Is it a fairy story?' asked Ned.

'Just let me get going and you'll see how grown up a story it is.'

'OK.' Ned pulled up the bedclothes higher and settled down to listen. It occurred to him that he was actually dreaming, but if so, at least he wasn't frightened any more.

'Once upon a time, a war was being fought throughout the world,' Mab began again. 'Millions of people had already been killed when our story starts. In the country we're particularly concerned with, bombs had fallen in many of the big cities so that, whenever possible, children were sent away to the countryside, which was safer.

'After four years of fighting, our side was beginning to win. It was possible to see a brighter, peaceful future.

'Then the enemy invented a new kind of bomb, more a rocket really, which flew swiftly over the city. As it approached it made a horrible whining noise like a giant insect. When it became silent a massive explosion followed and whole streets with men, women and children living in them were blown apart.'

'I bet this is World War II,' interrupted Ned. 'The city's London and the rockets were doodlebugs.'

'This is just the *setting*, clever-clogs,' said Mab a little bossily. 'Now the real story part gets going.' She took a breath. 'In the city lived a young girl called Maybelle. Her father was a soldier and had been away fighting abroad for two years. Her mother worked in a canteen and was very busy.

'When the V1s or doodlebugs appeared, Maybelle's mother decided it was too dangerous for her daughter to stay in the city.

'Maybelle pleaded, "Please, Mummy, let me stay with you. I promise you I'll go down to the shelter whenever we hear the siren."

' "The trouble is, Maybelle, my nerves are in shreds with the horrible noise and the thought that you might be the one blown to pieces. But I promise you I've had an idea you'll like."

'Maybelle's mother had been married twice and had a daughter, by her first husband, called Melanie. She was twenty years old and worked as a land girl on the east coast.'

'What's a land girl?' asked Ned.

'Just what it sounds like. Someone who works on the land, helping to produce food for the troops and everyone else. Anyway, Maybelle's mother knew

Maybelle hero-worshipped her half-sister so it was a very clever idea.

'"Oh, Mum," said Maybelle, "can I really live with Melanie?"

'"That's what I'm saying. She's lucky. She's not with the other girls, she's got her own little cottage, so there's room for another. You'll have to behave yourself."

'Filled with excitement, Maybelle travelled to join her elder sister. And, if Melanie wasn't very keen, that's only natural, isn't it? Being saddled with a little kid, even if it is your sister.'

'I'm going to be saddled with a brother or sister soon,' said Ned in a self-pitying voice.

'I wish you wouldn't keep interrupting.' This time Mab sounded quite cross. 'It breaks up the mood of the story.'

'Sorry.'

'So. Maybelle lived in the little cottage on the edge of the sea and, because it was school holidays, she'd plenty of time to play. Gradually she realised that Melanie had another life outside the farm where she worked and the cottage. She'd set off early evening, all smartened with red lipstick and hair rolled high in the front.

'Maybelle asked her where she was going but she wouldn't say. "You're too young," she told her. "I'm always back before it's dark, aren't I?"

'"Oh yes. I'm not complaining," said Maybelle. She was just curious because she loved her sister and wanted to understand her.

'Then one day, she looked out of her little bedroom window, facing the sea, and saw a Jeep drive up. The next moment, Melanie had jumped out and, blowing a kiss to the man at the wheel, came into the house.

'Now the secret was out. Melanie had a boyfriend. An American airman! Maybelle had been around quite long enough to recognise the uniform.

'She dashed downstairs and confronted her sister, who was sitting on the sofa in the front sitting-room. "You've got a boyfriend! And he's off the US air base!"

'To Maybelle's total surprise, Melanie burst into tears. "Oh, May, I'm so scared! I love him so much. But every day, he goes off on these raids – sometimes twice a day – and it's so dangerous. And we're engaged, but he won't let me tell anyone in case he doesn't come back one time and he doesn't want me tied or mourning him all my life . . . and I'm so frightened for him . . ."

'After that she couldn't do anything but cry, and I held her as tight as I could. I felt like her big sister instead of the other way round.

'"Don't worry, Melanie," I told her, "I'll look after you." And I stroked her hair and found a handkerchief to dry her eyes.

'From then on, we were very very close. She told me everything. Of course, she couldn't tell our mother. The airman, who was called Doug, didn't want her to, and in those days it wasn't done to have a real boyfriend unless you were engaged. Anyway, she didn't want to give my mother more worries. It was

35

enough she had my father at the front and doodlebugs at home.

'I could look after Melanie – at least when she was back in the cottage. When Doug was out on a bombing raid, Melanie lay awake worrying all night long. Sometimes she'd make herself a cup of tea and I'd get up too and we'd play Prince's Quest until dawn came and she'd set off for the farm.

'By September I was going to the little village school. One good thing, my mother wrote and told us the doodlebugs were hardly getting through any more so we didn't have to be quite so anxious about her.

'This went on for a couple of months. Soon the evenings became dark early and Melanie was home when I got back from school. It was one dark afternoon in November that a motorcycle came up the road with a roar. There was a knock at the door.

'We guessed he was bringing a telegram and we knew what that meant. Melanie immediately assumed Doug had been lost – but of course no one would have sent *us* a telegram about him.

'Anyway, it had to be me who opened the little yellow envelope and drew out the paper inside. I read the two lines several times.

'"Melanie, it's not about Doug. It's Mum. She's been killed in a rocket attack." I was clenching my fists so hard to stop myself crying that my nails drew blood.

'Later we found out it was a new sort of rocket that killed her – a V2. This one didn't make any noise at all. I said to Melanie, "At least Mum wouldn't have known it was coming." We both knew how she hated the whiny noise of the doodlebugs. I was trying to be strong for both of us.

'But Melanie wouldn't be comforted. She was an orphan now, with her father dead long ago. And not long after, *my* father was killed too. In Italy, they said. So we only had each other.

'Melanie was more and more sure that Doug would be next. She wouldn't eat and she didn't sleep, and the only time she was happy was when she was with Doug.

' "You've got to keep cheerful for him," I told her, like the big sister again.

' "I will try," she said, "but I'm just waiting, waiting for the news he's gone too."

'The cruel thing was, she turned out to be right. Doug flew out with his squadron one December night, cold and black without a star or a moon, and he never came back.

'People were dying all over. But Melanie took it personally. She even seemed to blame herself for the deaths. In fact, she went right out of her mind. She told the farm she was ill and barely got out of bed.

'Ned,' Mab interrupted herself in her story. 'Ned, are you still awake?'

'Oh, yes.' He paused. 'It's a very sad story, Mab. And why are you talking about it? As if it was your story?'

Mab paused a moment but didn't answer Ned's question.

'There were lots of sad stories in the war. This story gets even sadder.'

'Don't stop,' said Ned.

'Here goes,' said Mab. 'Then one day – a wild, windy day, with sleety rain blowing in from the sea – I got home from school and Melanie wasn't there.

'It wasn't the sort of house you could hide in, except up the loft, so I climbed up with a torch but there was no sign of her. It wasn't the day for a walk either, it was dark already and bitterly cold. Besides, her coat was on the peg in the hall.

'I waited hours, getting more and more anxious. I knew she must have gone out. The wind was rising high, shrieking round the windows and doors, sometimes sounding quite piteously like someone calling for help.

'I began to believe it was Melanie's voice, joining with the wind to call me out.

'So I put on my coat and hat and gloves and set out. The wind nearly knocked me over. I looked towards the sea. At first it was only blackness and noise, then the clouds, racing on the wind, parted for a moment. A full moon lit up the scene.

'I'd never seen the sea so tossed about. As if someone was whipping it up like cream in a bowl. Which is just what the wind was doing. The peaks were as high as mountains – moving mountains, advancing on me like an army.'

'Like tonight,' put in Ned. 'The sea's like that tonight. I saw it from the window.'

'Well, I wished I was safely in my bed, like we are. But I knew I had to find Melanie, so I carried on. I was bent almost double against the wind. I had reached the wooden sheds where the fishermen kept their nets—'

'It's here. It happened here!' cried Ned excitedly.

'Sshh . . . The clouds parted once again. The moon shone directly down like a vast spotlight. What I saw filled me with terror.

'"Melanie! Melanie!" I ran towards the sea. She was there in the waves, her long hair streaming in the wind. Any moment she would be knocked down and disappear under the mass of water. She was walking deliberately into deeper water. I knew if the water got above knee-height I'd never get her back.

'I ran across the beach and into the icy water. It was like pushing against weights to put one leg in front of the other. Slowly I forced myself to her side. I grabbed her arm and screamed in her ear, "No! Melanie. No! Turn round! Come home!"

'Her face was pale as the moon, her eyes fixed and unseeing. Around us the angry water frothed and swirled. "It's me, Maybelle! Look at me."

'And she did. Just before the clouds closed over the moon again, she gave me a little smile. She had changed her mind. She turned round and started for the shore. She was safe! I had saved her.

'But as she began to wade to shore, the sea boiled up in a fearful rage as if determined to take revenge for losing a victim. A huge wave came steamrolling in.

'Melanie was already in shallow water but I was

39

behind her and smaller. The wave overwhelmed me like a towering mountain, curled over my body, drowned me utterly, then took my body out to sea. Melanie was safe but I was never seen again.'

There was a pause; Ned tried to understand. 'You drowned? You, yourself?'

'That's right.'

There was something very odd about this story. It had begun as the story of a girl called Maybelle but, halfway through, the 'she' had changed to 'I'.

'Maybelle is the same person as Mab Angel!' he whispered.

'I thought you'd guessed earlier.'

'But if you're Maybelle and Maybelle drowned . . .' Ned felt very confused.

'If you're going to say what I think you're going to say—'

'You're a ghost!'

'Don't sound so miserable. The dying's all behind me – sixty years ago and more. Now I'm a very kind, cheerful ghost.' She paused and said more gently, 'You see, I couldn't let Ellen be lonely, could I?'

'Ellen . . . Melanie,' murmured Ned.

'Not after I'd persuaded her to come out of the waves. I had to keep up her spirits. I didn't come all the time. Just when she needed me. Mostly on wild nights or when she felt sad and lonely. We played games, that sort of thing.'

'And tonight you came to visit me.' Ned found his voice was becoming very small. He was beginning

to feel very very tired. It had been a long story –
a long night.

'I think it's time you went to sleep.'

'Sometimes you sound more like a grown-up than
a girl.'

'I've been around a long time, one way and another.'

Ned sensed she was smiling but her voice seemed to
be coming from a long way away. 'You will come back,
won't you?'

'If you need me.'

And that was the very last thing Ned heard that
night as he slipped into a deep sleep.

7

He woke with sun on his face and a friendly Sid kneading the bedclothes with her claws.

'Hi, Sid. Want your breakfast, do you?' Then he remembered. He sat bolt-upright.

The storm had completely vanished. He could hear the calm swishing of the waves keeping time with Sid's purring. But it wasn't just the storm Ned remembered.

Mab Angel. There'd been a girl called Mab here with him last night. Or was it a dream?

'OK Sid, I'm coming.' Ned put his legs out of bed and it was then he realised that he had been *sleeping the wrong end of the bed*. And the reason for that was that Mab Angel had been at the head.

Ned went downstairs with Sid tangling around his legs. He remembered how frightened he'd been the night before and how quickly he'd fallen asleep after Mab had stayed with him.

Yet in the bright morning it was hard to believe it had happened. She'd told him a sad story too, more like a nightmare really, all about deaths and drowning. Although she'd seemed quite cheerful.

He went to the larder for a tin of cat food and noticed at once that the window was open. But he knew he'd closed it. He remembered clearly shutting it tightly to keep out the wind. Someone must have been here. Even Sid, clever though she was, couldn't have let herself out.

Ned opened the cat food thoughtfully and then noticed something else. The game he'd been playing the night before, Prince's Quest, had gone. He went quickly into the living-room, opened the cupboard and there it was, packed neatly away with all the other games.

Obviously, Mab Angel had looked after things last night. The knowledge gave him a sense of comfort and security. He wasn't alone any longer.

Passing back through the hallway to the kitchen, Ned suddenly saw a letter on the mat. It gave him a fright, even though it could only be post for poor old Aunt Ellen.

He picked up the letter and was shocked to find that it was addressed to Mr Edward Fairley. But that was him! Could his parents have sent it?

Nervously, he took it to the kitchen and sat down at the table. Sid immediately jumped on to his lap. 'You're such a lump, Sid!' It was good putting it off. But he had to open the letter. With a sinking heart, he tore the envelope and took out sheet of typed paper.

It came from the hospital. The hospital wished to inform Mr Edward Fairley, as next of kin to Miss Ellen

Mary Clementine Fairley, that the said lady was a patient in the hospital, having suffered a stroke.

It continued to inform him that she was in intensive care and that, although she had been able to indicate his existence at an early stage, her situation had deteriorated and at present she was unable to talk or even write.

Ned read the letter several times. He felt really sorry for his aunt. But he was also surprised by it. It was not at all the sort of letter a hospital would write to a schoolboy. If they thought he was alone at his age they'd have come to get him at once.

Gradually, he worked out what had probably happened. Aunt Ellen had managed to tell them his name before her 'situation deteriorated' but not his age. They thought he was an adult. All he had to do was lie low.

But then something else struck him. Surely they would expect him to visit the hospital? That gave him another problem. He got up and found a packet of biscuits in the larder. He'd eaten half of them before the answer hit him. Brilliant! He went back to the front room and over to a little desk, then pulled out drawers until he found writing-paper and envelopes, a pen and stamps. It was quite simple: he would write and say, as if he was a grown-up, that he had flu but would come as soon as he was better.

It was a perfect morning. Ned left the house in search of a post box with Sid following behind.

He held the envelope protectively inside his pocket. He felt confident and in control. After he'd posted the letter, he'd walk along the sea front and explore the effects of the storm.

He reached the road leading back into the village and, as he turned into it, he was tempted to pull the hood of his jacket up. It would make him anonymous but, on the other hand, it might raise suspicions. Better not.

In a few moments he was in the main street, such as it was. He spotted a small pub called the Admiral's Poop which advertised rooms, a bow-fronted window which seemed to be a café, and a general store with a post box outside on the pavement.

'Go away, Sid.' He waved his arms. She easily might be recognised as Great-Aunt Ellen's cat. Getting the point at once, Sid found the brightest spot of sunlight and sat down demurely.

Ned hurried forward. Just as he neared the box, two women came out of the store carrying shopping bags and stopped opposite it. He could see they were planning on a good chat.

'The wind cut through the walls like a knife,' said one.

'There were no boats out, I hope?'

'There're always some young fools who don't believe in weather warnings. At least we don't have the fishing fleet to worry about any more.'

'The tragedies we've seen!'

'Some people don't pay the sea proper respect, that's the truth.'

Clearly, they weren't in a hurry to move so Ned had no choice but to make a dash for it.

'Morning, dear,' said one woman as he dropped the letter into the box. Ned didn't answer.

It was a relief to get back to the sea front. There was no one to ask him awkward questions there.

He headed for the boat and the wooden huts, curious whether the waves had surged that high the night before. At first glance the sea seemed calm enough but as he went closer, he could see that the smooth surface hid a huge swell. It was as if the storm had gone underground, waiting to come out again when the time was right.

He moved backwards. Vague memories of Mab's story came to him. He felt suddenly cold, although the sun was as bright as ever. Perhaps he'd go back to the warmth and safety of Lilac Cottage and leave the boats for later.

'Come on, Sid!' He called to the cat, who was following him as usual at a distance. 'Home we go!'

They walked back side by side.

He didn't know what made him turn suddenly to look at one of the houses as he passed. Maybe it was a creepy awareness of being watched because, as he turned, he saw a face staring out: a strange old face, dark and wrinkled, with a wiry white beard and bushy eyebrows. Then it was gone, wooden shutters closed firmly across the window.

'Just some stupid old bat,' he told Sid. But the sight

had unnerved him and he was even gladder to open Lilac Cottage's front door and breathed a sigh of relief as he went straight through to the kitchen.

But there another surprise awaited him. Because he'd woken late and been in a hurry to write the letter to the hospital and get it posted, he'd left the kitchen in a bit of a mess.

He could picture how it'd been: a loaf of bread on the table, along with butter, jam, a packet of cereal and a bottle of milk. They'd been in a little group. Now it looked as if an animal had jumped on to the table, knocking over the cereal packet, spilling milk.

What animal could use a bread knife? Someone had cut several pieces of bread – in fact there was hardly any left – and had at least two full bowls of cereal, plus all the milk.

Whoever it was had been voraciously hungry! He tried not to be frightened. Nevertheless he went upstairs with his heart beating uncomfortably fast. Would he find a wild person, a burglar, a murderer even?

He looked round his bedroom first, under the bed, under the bedclothes, in the cupboard. The room was quite empty and the sun beamed in cheerfully.

Could it be the mysterious Mab Angel come back? Making a mess like that in the kitchen didn't seem at all like the girl he'd met, and anyway she'd told him she usually came at night.

So then he went to search his aunt's room. But there was nothing there either.

Just the living-room now, before he could relax.

There were plenty of cupboards – every one filled and no room for even the smallest person to hide.

Back in the kitchen, Sid stood persuasively over her empty bowl. 'Hang on, Sid. I'm getting to you.' As he found a tin of cat food, he decided that there were only two ways the intruder could have got in: either through the front door with a key – not very likely. Or through the little window he'd used himself – which gave him a clue.

'It's either a monkey, a dwarf or a child,' he told Sid as he fed her. 'I've got to find out where he's come from before all our supplies disappear.'

'Miaow!' responded Sid warmly, and began to eat nearly as hungrily as the intruder.

'After lunch, we'll go on a recce.'

But somehow after lunch, Ned didn't feel very energetic. Instead of going out, he got out his discman and decided to relax with a bit of *White Stripes*.

It's extraordinary how quickly time passes when you're doing nothing. He might not have left the comfort of Lilac Cottage at all, except that just when he'd pulled off his ear-phones, he suddenly heard footsteps at the back of the house.

Sid had heard them too. She was standing, legs braced, tail quivering. Then they both raced into the larder. The window was open, more than it had been before, and they could hear someone running away fast.

'Come on, Sid.' Without stopping to think further, Ned jumped on to the ledge and launched himself through the window. It was much easier getting out than it had been getting in.

8

The evening light was dimming fast as Ned, followed by Sid, sped out of the little back garden and on to the sea front.

The intruder had got a good start on them and must be running very fast because he was only the vaguest of shadows, occasionally silhouetted against the greater brightness of the sea and sky. Then even that turned black and the figure disappeared altogether.

Ned stopped to get his breath. He bent double, panting hard, and came face to face with Sid's gleaming green eyes.

'Where's he gone, then, Sid? I bet you could show me.'

The cat's tail went up and she began to walk in a purposeful manner.

Since there seemed nothing else to do, Ned followed her. Soon they'd passed the last house and were heading towards the boats.

'We're not going to sea, I hope?' joked Ned.

The cat continued, going fast now, until they'd reached the wooden sheds where Mab had said the fishermen used to hang their nets. She went straight to the third shed and stood there growling.

'You're a tiger, Sid.' Ned bent down to stroke her and to get his nerve back. Clearly, Sid believed the intruder was in the shed – unless it was rats, as he'd thought before.

It was time to be brave. He banged on the door and shouted, 'Open up! I know you're in there!'

Absolute silence followed. Even Sid had stopped pretending to be a tiger. Ned wished it wasn't so very dark. He banged on the door again. 'You can't get away, so you might as well come out!'

Again there was complete silence. Then he heard a faint rustle inside. This time, instead of banging, he pushed on the door – and, to his surprise, it opened several centimetres before being abruptly halted. It was as if someone was holding it shut with their own weight and he remembered the same thing had happened the day before. It didn't feel like a very strong someone.

Ned took a few steps backwards and then ran at the door, pushing with all his might.

The door shot open and Ned found himself sprawled on the floor. Behind him he was aware of Sid at the entrance, as if to stop anyone escaping.

He sprang to his feet. It was far too dark to see anything but he could hear a scuffling in the corner. He decided to change his tactics. Perhaps this person was frightened too.

'Look, I'm not going to hurt you. I just want to know if you were stealing my food.'

The scuffling increased, followed by a very soft whisper. 'You won't tell on me, will you?'

Ned thought, with relief, the voice sounded like a child's, as he'd suspected. 'Who are you?'

'No one. I'm no one.'

'You have to be somebody.'

'No, I don't. Not if I don't want to. Have you got that cat with you? I like that cat.'

'So it *was* you who stole my food,' Ned said with satisfaction. It was nice to have that puzzle solved.

'It weren't stealing. Not really.'

'Well, I don't know how you work that out – but why don't you come here and we can talk properly.' Ned took a couple of steps in the direction of the corner.

'Only if you swear not to tell nobody.' The voice was louder but even more nervously suspicious.

'OK. But Sid knows already.'

'I told you, I like the cat.'

Clearly this boy was in no mood for jokes. Ned smiled into the darkness.

A small figure appeared at his side. 'So here I am, aren't I? What you going to do, now?' The voice sounded anxious and defiant at the same time.

Ned hadn't thought about this. 'How old are you?'

'What's that to you? Old enough.'

'I bet you're younger than me.'

'So what are you going to do with me?' repeated the intruder. 'You're not going to get the police?'

Ned thought. At the door Sid miaowed and twitched

her tail. There was just enough light behind her to see her take a couple of steps out.

The point was, he couldn't take the boy to the police because he was in hiding himself.

'You'd better come back with us.'

'To that old lady's house?'

Ned tried to see the boy's expression in the dark. 'How did you know an old lady lived there?'

'How do you think?' He sounded sulky. 'She gave me stuff to eat, didn't she? She didn't want me starving. I told you it wasn't stealing. I just had to get through the window when she wasn't there herself. Get me?'

'I get you,' replied Ned. 'Let's walk.' He was beginning to get the wider picture too.

As they walked back along the seashore, he straightened his thoughts. Obviously the boy was hiding out in the shed and Aunt Ellen, before she was taken to hospital, had given him food.

'What's your name?' he asked as they neared the cottage.

'What's it to you? Danny, if you must know.'

'So, Danny, are you going to tell me your story?'

But at that moment, Danny shot ahead along the pavement. Ned caught up with him, crouching by the gate to the back garden of Lilac Cottage.

'What's the matter?'

'Did you see him?' Danny sounded terrified. 'At the window. An old geezer. I've seen him watching before. I don't like him!'

'I can tell that.' Ned tried to sound brave, but

53

actually he remembered how unnerved he'd been by that old man's face staring from between the shutters. It had to be the same one. 'Let's get inside.'

This turned out to be easier said than done as, in his haste to chase the intruder – in other words, Danny – he'd forgotten the door keys.

In the end, they both had to climb in through the window all over again. Although smaller, Danny was very agile, and up and in quicker than Ned.

Ned switched on the kitchen light and for the first time he could see his guest.

'You look like Gollum!' He was so shocked he spoke without thinking. Danny was filthy. His face was swollen and blotchy, his hair – which grew almost to his shoulders – was matted and greasy with odd bits stuck in it, and his clothes were torn and jumbled on top of each other in no particular order. He even seemed to be wearing two pairs of trousers.

'You've no right to call me names!' Danny's fists were clenched and his dark eyes screwed up aggressively.

'Sorry.' As Ned looked closer, he saw that Danny was not only dirty and bedraggled but also covered in cuts and bruises. His left eye was half-closed with purplish-green swelling all around it. Better not mention it unless he wanted to set the boy off again. 'Now we're here, let's eat.'

'Nice one!'

Ned opened a tin of baked beans and fried up some bacon while Danny sniffed hungrily.

The moment they'd finished – Ned hadn't dared

suggest Danny wash first – Danny was up with an expectant expression.

'So where's the TV?'

'I thought you'd been here before. My great-aunt doesn't know about television. She doesn't want it anyway.'

'So she's your auntie, is she? What happened to her then? Where's she gone?'

'She's in hospital.'

Immediately, Danny's face took on the furtive, frightened expression Ned was beginning to recognise. 'So who's with you? Where's your mum and dad? I'm not staying here so they find me. She was all right, your aunt. She promised to keep me secret. She said she was good at secrets.'

By now Danny was half in the larder, ready to jump back out of the window. Ned grabbed his shoulder, noticing as he did so that Danny winced as if he were bruised there too. 'It's OK, honestly. I'm on my own.'

'You're not! A boy like you – you'd be looked after.'

'I promise you! My parents are away. I was supposed to be staying with my aunt but she was taken to hospital the evening I got here, so I stayed on my own. I don't want some interfering strangers looking after me. I'm laying low – which is what you're doing too, aren't you?'

Danny hesitated. 'Swear you won't give me away?'

'If I give you away I'd give myself away, and I don't want to do that.'

'I can stay here with you and nobody will know?'

55

Ned wasn't sure he had meant quite that, but there was no going back now. 'For a week or so anyway. On one condition.'

Danny, who was back in the kitchen, stopped dead. 'What?'

'You have a bath.' Ned laughed loudly and noticed with some relief that even Danny was smiling tentatively.

'There wasn't much water where I've been the last few days – apart from the sea. Even if it hadn't been as cold as ice, I can't swim.'

'You can swim in the bath now.'

'On my way, sir!' Danny saluted mockingly.

So Ned showed him up the stairs and hoped those cuts were healed enough not to sting. He must find out how Danny got them.

9

After Danny had gone up for his bath, Ned took out Prince's Quest and was quietly setting up the board on the floor of the front room when he heard the door open behind him. But Danny was still in the bath.

'Sid?'

'Sidonie's dozing in the kitchen,' said a girl's voice.

'Mab Angel!' Ned turned round delightedly. 'I thought you might not come back again. It's not even a wild night.'

'I always come when I'm needed.'

Ned didn't try and question this one. Besides, he was staring too hard at his visitor. Of course they'd only met in the dark. There was something odd about Mab's clothes. She was wearing a pleated skirt made of some heavy material, white ankle-length socks, blue button shoes, and a rather shrunken sweater with a pattern round the neck. Her hair was odd too: straight, not very long and parted precisely at the side, the longer portion held back by a blue slide.

She reminded him of something but he couldn't quite remember what.

'A cat may look at a queen,' said Mab in her nice accent, 'but there are limits.'

'Sorry.' Ned tried to turn his eyes away.

'I know.' Mab sounded more sympathetic. 'I look strange to you. But then you look strange to me, which makes us even-stevens.'

Ned looked down at what he was wearing. It seemed perfectly ordinary: baggy jeans, his favourite Nikes and a hoody with Bart Simpson on the back.

'So what's so funny about me?' Ned asked rather defensively.

'Well, your hair's quite a bit too long for one thing. In my day the barber would have the razor to it. Then your clothes, frankly, are silly. They don't make any sense at all. In fact you look a real mess. Where're your short trousers, long socks, lace-up leather shoes, flannel shirt and pullover?'

Ned could see Mab wasn't being too serious, so he decided to give her some of her own medicine. 'You look like something out of a history book—' He began, and then stopped abruptly. That was what she reminded him of: photos of children during World War II – and that was exactly where she'd come from. He felt himself gasping for air like a fish.

Mab laughed at his expression. 'Yes. Yes,' she said eventually. 'Just because I seem to be standing here in front of you, it doesn't mean I've stopped being a ghost.'

Ned took in her matter-of-fact tone. This wasn't someone playing games. This was for real. 'It's just that I've never met a g-ghost before,' he stammered out.

'You didn't seem so shocked last night,' said Mab just a little reproachfully.

'I was half asleep. You might have been a d-dream.'

'A dream, am I now?' Mab sat on a chair and swung her legs crossly. 'I don't know why I bothered to tell you the story of my life – and death – if that's all you can come up with.'

Ned made up his mind. 'I'm sorry. Really I am. You're all right.' He got up from the floor and went over to her. 'Course I believe in you. I saw you'd shut the window and put away Prince's Quest. It just takes a bit of getting used to.'

Mab crossed her arms but seemed a little mollified. 'It's true Ellen shrieked when she first saw me. At least you didn't shriek.'

'Yes,' agreed Ned, and he thought it best not to point out that the reason he hadn't shrieked – not that he ever shrieked anyway – when she first appeared was because, unlike Great-Aunt Ellen, he hadn't known she was already drowned.

'Anyway, this is boring!' cried Mab, jumping off the chair and clapping her hands. 'What's our plan?'

'Our plan?' asked Ned. He still felt a bit unsure. And she was so confident.

'Yes. Plan. Your visitor upstairs. What are we going to do about her?'

'Danny? Are you talking about Danny?'

59

'Of course I'm talking about Danny. I mean so far so good. You've rescued her from starvation and worse, but now we've got to look to the future.'

Ned sat down slowly on the chair just vacated by Mab. He thought that it was very difficult dealing with someone who always seemed to be one step ahead of him. 'What do you mean "her"? Danny's a boy. I saw her – that is, him.'

Mab laughed merrily, making Ned reflect that the common perception of ghosts as mournful creatures, drifting about making weird moaning sounds, was certainly wrong if Mab was anything to go by.

'Danielle, silly. Danny for short. Do you want me to take you up to the bathroom and prove it?'

'It's not a joke, Mab . . .' Ned felt himself going red. Surely sixty-year-old ghosts shouldn't make that sort of suggestion.

'Incidentally, just a tip. Why don't you think of me as a *visitor from the past* instead of a ghost?' She made a face.

So now she's reading my mind as well as everything else, thought Ned. But there was no doubt that things were livelier with Mab around, his own personal visitor from the past. He tried the term to himself and liked it.

'OK. She's a girl. You know best.' He heard his voice bright and positive. 'But do you know how she got all those cuts and bruises?'

'That's just why I'm back. She's more likely to tell me, one girl to another.'

'So you don't want me to confront her?'

'Certainly not. You can do the washing-up or something while I talk to her. Meanwhile let's play Prince's Quest. Bags I the yellow knight.'

Half an hour and more passed. For fifteen minutes of this, Ned's red knight was lost in the Dark Wood. When he finally came out the other side, he remembered Danny. Surely she/he couldn't still be in the bath?

'I'm going up!' he told Mab. 'Maybe something's wrong.'

'I thought we'd agreed . . .' began Mab but Ned was already up the stairs, calling at the bathroom door.

'Danny! Are you in there? Danny!' There was no answer. Seriously worried, he knocked loudly. Still no answer. Tentatively, he turned the handle and found himself in an empty room. He/she had had a bath all right, the filthy ring proved it. And there was a pile of dirty clothes on the floor.

Ned hurried into his own room. The chest of drawers was open, T-shirts and trousers on the floor. Clearly Danny had picked a new outfit for himself. (Ned decided he was going to assume Danny was a boy until proved otherwise, whatever Mab said.) This was stealing, no other word for it. Thinking of the desperate state in which he'd found Danny, he supposed it should be no surprise. But he did feel let down all the same.

He checked his aunt's room, but in his bones he felt sure Danny had gone. He and Mab had been so engrossed in their game, Danny could have walked out through the front door without them hearing. He'd enjoyed a good meal, a bath, kitted himself out in clean clothes and scarpered.

Slowly, Ned went downstairs and into the front room.

'He's gone!'

'Gone – whatever do you mean?' Mab jumped up.

'Gone. Vanished. Vamoosed. Ejected. Gone into orbit.'

'I don't know what you're talking about, but you've got to go after her.'

Ned sat down. 'He stole my clothes.'

'So? She must have needed them.'

Although this was more or less Ned's approach, he suddenly felt obstinate. 'I try to help him and then he repays me by stealing my favourite sweatshirt.' Actually this wasn't true; it was an old sweatshirt he'd never much liked. 'He's probably pinched food too. I don't see why I should bother for someone like him.'

'Her,' said Mab. She sat down again. 'I know you'll help her. You know what it's like to be alone and frightened.'

'Why don't you go yourself, if you're so keen?' said Ned sulkily.

'Because I can't. That's why.'

'Well, I can't either.'

There was a silence. Ned felt guilty and horrid and very anxious about Danny out there in the dark. He'd been so scared in that shed. And there were all those cuts and bruises. He looked at Mab. She was fiddling with a strand of hair, twirling it around, then letting it go before catching it again and re-starting the process.

'Why can't *you* go?' Ned knew he would go and look for Danny. He was just putting off entering the dark night a little longer.

'I told you I was a visitor from the past. Well, this is where I visit. I can't go anywhere except Lilac Cottage. So let's face it, Danny's fate is in your hands.'

'But you'll be here when I get back?'

'If you need me.'

'Yes.'

'Cross my heart and hope to die,' said Mab, which seemed to Ned the silliest choice of words possible.

Ned left through the front door boldly. It was a good bet that Danny would go back to his hiding-place in the shed. Ned ran most of the way there, so that he was thoroughly puffed out by the time he arrived.

'Danny! It's me!'

But he knew at once there was no one there. In the quiet darkness, the door swung on its hinges with a squawking noise.

Ned walked back slowly. Danny couldn't have gone far and he certainly wouldn't have headed to the village where someone might see him. He wondered if Mab might be the reason Danny had run away. Perhaps he thought Ned had lied when he said he was on his own. Of course he hadn't counted on a ghost – sorry, a visitor from the past!

Ned began to feel even more worried about Danny. Should he search the other way, along the sea front?

Suddenly he heard a shrill cry and a scream. 'Let go! Let me go!' Then silence.

10

Ned was running again. Once again he was terrified and out of breath. He knew it had been Danny screaming and he suspected it had come from the direction of the house where the old man watched from behind the shutters.

He slowed and approached the house warily. He tried to remind himself that Mab was waiting for him in Lilac Cottage only a few metres down the road, but he couldn't help feeling very much alone. Even Sid had deserted him recently.

He could hear his heavy breathing and as it quietened, the soft waves behind him. Imagining all sorts of horrors, Ned crept forward. Then he heard voices. A deep man's mostly. The front door of the house was open, throwing a glimmer of light on to the pavement.

His eyes adjusted more and he saw two figures close together. He couldn't hear what the old man was saying but the tone was questioning, the same sounds repeated several times and always with a lift at the end.

It didn't seem angry or threatening but Ned could still hear Danny's screams in his head. Maybe he was tied and gagged!

If only his dad was here. He was big and strong enough to take on two or three crazy old men. In fact any large grown-up person would have done. For the first time Ned began to regret cutting himself off from the ordinary world.

At least surprise was on his side – the old man was far too involved to notice anything else. Best thing was to take a deep breath, then attack with as much noise as possible.

Just as Ned was reciting to himself: 'One, two, three . . .' he noticed that Sid had joined him, a large black shadow. Somehow the sight gave him courage.

'One, two, three, GO!' Shouting at the top of his voice, arms flailing like a windmill, Ned rushed forward. Instantly, the two figures separated, revealing a tall but immensely old figure, gaunt and bent, a stick in one hand.

At that moment, Sid leaped with a wild caterwaul, aiming with the precision of a military missile straight at the old man's legs.

As he tangled with his stick in a desperate effort to stay upright, Danny dashed to Ned's side.

'Don't hang around!' shouted Ned. 'Head for the cottage!'

Danny obeyed and they both ran like whirlwinds, followed closely by Sid, who naturally went for the larder window as Ned fumbled with the keys for the front door.

'Quick! He might be following!' Ned could feel Danny panting beside him.

They got through the door safely and into the kitchen. But just as Ned was heaving a sigh of relief, Danny let out a shriek. 'There's still someone here! You promised me! You said there was no one. Only you.'

'Take it easy, Danny.' Ned grabbed his arm. 'This is Mab Angel. Mab Angel – Danny. Danny – Mab Angel. She's, she's . . .' Ned hesitated. It seemed a bit difficult to explain what she was. 'She's one of us.' Which certainly wasn't true.

Danny was still pulling at his arm, but Ned held on tightly as Mab approached, smiling. If only she didn't look so odd, thought Ned anxiously. Her button shoes were really bizarre.

'My name's Mab,' said Mab, holding out her hand as if she wanted to shake hands (another oddity). 'I promise I won't hurt you nor tell anyone where you are.'

Ned noticed too that her way of speaking was much more precise than his and even more different from Danny's.

'I was that scared when I heard another voice,' said Danny, 'so I ran off. Then that monster nabbed me. I was coming back to look through your window. See what I could see. You don't know what it's like sleeping rough. Then this big hand was on my shoulder. He may be old but he's strong all right.'

'Come and sit down,' said Mab soothingly. 'I'll make us a nice cup of tea.'

'Tea?' questioned Ned, but Danny seemed pleased enough.

'Two sugars and a biscuit. You're fine, you, Mab. I like you.'

'That's good,' said Ned, although to tell the truth he felt a little left out. After all, he'd been the one to rescue him.

Nevertheless, he had to admit with a warm cup of tea in his hand (a drink he usually detested) and the three of them sitting round the table with Sid making a big deal about lapping at a saucer of milk, it did feel cosy.

'So what happened out there?' he asked. 'Why did the old man grab you? What did he say to you?'

Danny looked down into his cup without answering.

'Give the girl a chance.' Mab looked at Ned reproachfully.

'And what's all this "girl" business?' Ned felt cross all over again.

'It takes a girl to know a girl,' said Mab smugly.

'You're not a girl! You're a . . . a . . .' Ned stopped.

'Don't know what it's to do with anything,' Danny looked up, 'but, as it happens, she hit the spot.'

'You're all such liars!' exclaimed Ned with disgust.

Danny flared up at once. 'I never said I was a boy! You just decided it. I expect most of your friends are boys so you turned me into one. It's Danielle, see.

Danny's what I've always been called. So you shut it!'
Now she seemed near tears.

Ned felt ashamed. He would have liked another boy.
There were no two ways about it. With all the
excitement of Danny's capture and escape, he hadn't
really looked at her since she'd washed – but now he
saw she was quite clearly a girl. Her hair, which he had
thought long for a boy, was the right length for a girl.
It was still, he noticed, tangled and dirty. Perhaps she'd
heard Mab's voice before she'd had a chance to wash it.
Of course Great-Aunt Ellen's bathroom didn't run to a
shower.

'Sorry.' Ned thought what he could say to prove it.
'How come you're living rough and all that?'

'Life's rough, isn't it?' Danny's face was closed.

Ned had felt pretty sorry for himself seeing his aunt
going off and being left all alone, but he couldn't
exactly say living in Lilac Cottage with plenty of food
and drink, a bed and other comforts (even if there
wasn't a television) was exactly 'rough'.

'So what was the old man on about?'

'Made no sense. Like when he got hold of me, he
seemed really nervous. I was scared rigid, of course.
But he was trying to be kind I think.'

'We all know about kind old men,' Mab interrupted
severely.

Ned felt surprised that they had that sort of 'kind
old man' in Mab's day, but nodded wisely.

'Not that way. I can't quite explain.' Danny frowned.
'He wasn't really interested in *me*, just that he wanted

69

to ask me something. He gave me chocolate fingers.'

'You didn't eat them, I hope!' exclaimed Mab.

'He said his teeth weren't so good and he liked sucking them so the chocolate came off and the biscuit part went soft.'

'Disgusting!' said Mab.

'Suppose.' Danny seemed less sure. 'I was terrified but he didn't do anything bad.'

'Apart from grabbing you in the first place,' said Ned indignantly. 'You were scared enough when you got away.'

'He wanted to ask me things. About this place. Lilac Cottage, he called it. He's squatting in that house. No electricity, no proper nothing. He's been there for a while. I don't know how long but he saw your auntie carried away. He got in a right old state about that.'

'Pleased, you mean?' asked Ned. 'He wanted it empty so he could get in and pinch all her stuff?' Privately he thought there wasn't much stuff to pinch.

'Funny sort of burglar,' commented Mab.

'More like Father Christmas with that beard,' Ned said, beginning to giggle. 'He'd never get a mask over it.'

'And he'd be picked out easy as anything in a police line-up,' added Danny, also beginning to giggle.

Soon they were all falling about with laughter, fuelled by a certain amount of hysteria following the tensions of the last few hours.

By the time they'd recovered, it seemed more important to prepare a hearty supper than solve the riddle of the old man. They were safe, and he could wait till the morning. Perhaps he'd disappear in the night and they'd never have to think about him again.

After supper, they moved into the front room and Ned got out Prince's Quest to show Danny but, somehow, none of them felt like playing it.

Ned looked at Danny curled into one of the armchairs. 'Danny, why *are* you running away? It's not just nosiness. Maybe I can help . . .'

'Ned means he wants your story,' said Mab quietly.

'You two wouldn't understand. It's my life, isn't it? Not a story.' Danny touched the worst cut on her cheek and winced.

'We don't mean story in that way. It's just that something dreadful must have happened. We want to be your friends. We want to know what's wrong.'

'It's a game to you.' Danny turned her face away.

'We want to *help*,' repeated Mab.

'No one can help. You don't know . . .' Her eyes glistened with tears. She blinked them back. 'You two could never understand my life.' Then she seemed to make up her mind. 'Oh, what's to lose. How do I start then?'

'Once upon a time . . .' prompted Mab.

11

'Once upon a time—' Danny broke off. 'Sounds stupid to me.'

'Go on!' encouraged Mab and Ned.

'You're such bullies. Oh, OK. So – once upon a time, there was a girl called Danielle. She lived with her mother – her father had done a runner when she was a baby – in a port town on the North Sea. It was a hard place to live – not much work for Danny's mum, cold east winds every day more or less – but she didn't expect anything different. Her mum got fed up, though. She wanted to have good times before she was too old. Some evenings after she'd been out for a drink, she'd say to Danny, "It's you put me into this fix. Don't you forget it. I could have got rid of you anytime, but, more fool me, I thought having a daughter'd be like in the films. I took pity on you. Stupidest thing I ever did."'

'Your mum sounds mean,' Ned said. His mum and dad might not be around much but they'd never say anything like that. 'No wonder you left.'

72

'You've got it all wrong.' Danny frowned at Ned. 'Tell the truth, I felt sorry for Mum. I must have been stupid too. Do you want to hear the rest or have a chat instead?'

'Course we want to hear,' chorused Ned and Mab.

'Anyway, Mum started having boyfriends. She'd often had the odd one, not lasting too long, not noticeable-like, round the house. But suddenly there seemed a different man every time I turned round. They took no notice of me but I still hated it. They were always drinking too.'

'My mum and dad drink,' said Ned.

'Not like this lot, I'll bet. Drinking to get drunk. So when Phil came along and seemed to be the one and only, I was glad at first. I even thought it was like having a dad. He drove us on trips along the coast. In his lorry. That was fun, sitting high up in the cab. I waved out of the window like I was famous until Mum stopped it.'

Danny interrupted herself this time and looked at Ned. 'Nasty story, like I said. And it gets worse. You see, my mum started being cross all the time, not just when she'd had a glass too many.

'Then Phil told me, quite nicely, "You're going to have a little brother or sister." He said, proud-like, although I knew he'd been married already and had children.

'I was shocked, more sensible than him as it turned out. "My mum doesn't like babies," I told him. "She didn't want me so why would she want another?"

'But he just laughed. I expect he thought his kid would be special. Men are dumb like that.

'Anyway, it was just as I expected. Mum hated being sick and fat. She wouldn't give up smoking or drinking whatever Phil said. She'd shout, "If you do, I will," but of course he wouldn't, so she didn't neither.

'She was lucky really because the baby was a beautiful little girl: bright eyes, fair curly hair. They called her Antoinette. It's a pretty name – but they weren't pleased with her at all because she should have been Anthony, a boy. It turned out Phil had three girls dotted about already.

'I was the one who liked Antoinette best – which was just as well, as I was the one who looked after her most, giving her a bottle in the night, that sort of thing. She'd say "mama" to me, not to my mum.'

'She loved you, didn't she?' said Mab.

Danny looked at her wearily. 'She was only little. It was hard in term-time, though. I had to get up Tony – I called her Tony, see – because Mum wouldn't be up, so I'd be late for school and the teachers'd come down on me. Then I got back and Mum was freaking out, saying I'd dawdled to make her late – although she'd just be going out to the local. So then I couldn't do my homework and they'd come down on me again, threaten to get my mum in for a talk. But she'd never have gone.'

'Didn't you have parents' evenings?' Ned put in. Not that his parents had been around for many of those.

Danny didn't even try to answer him. She went on

in a dull, monotonous voice, 'Phil got worse too. If Tony gave one little scream he'd be on to me like a ton of bricks, swearing and cursing. He went at my mum, telling her she was an unfit mother – which she was too, but he didn't have to hit her. He was tired, that was part of it, driving that lorry for hours and hours – right up to Scotland sometimes – driving, driving all hours of the day and night, and then coming back to a madhouse. That's what he called it – a madhouse, and he wasn't so wrong. With him in a temper and Tony crying and Mum screeching it was like a madhouse all right.

'I'd try and take Tony out then, whatever the time. Get out of his way, you know. The funny thing was, Tony's a real good baby. Like a little doll. I've never known her cry without reason, if you know what I mean.'

Danny stopped talking abruptly. Ned and Mab looked at each other anxiously. They could see Danny had tears in her eyes and was trying very hard not to cry.

Mab went over and put her hand on Danny's shoulder. 'Don't go on, if it upsets you.'

'No. I want to. I want you to know it all. Now I've got this far.' Danny sniffed noisily and wiped her eyes with her hands. Sid, appearing silently from somewhere or other, jumped on her lap and, after turning a couple of times, settled down and began to purr.

'Are we nearly at the end of the story?' asked Ned gently.

'Suppose.' Danny stroked Sid, as if to soothe herself more than the cat. 'It was four nights ago it happened. The worst thing. A nasty chill night. Mum and Phil had gone out drinking of course, which they called relaxing. Phil had just been told he had no work for a month or more so he wasn't in the best of moods. Usually, I didn't mind. It was the last day of school so I was in no rush. I had a routine for Tony too: play, bath, bottle, bed. Most times she'd be down by eight or nine. If she was wakeful we'd watch a bit of telly together.

'I could see there was something wrong when I got in. She was red and whimpery, not like herself. Mum said she'd kept nothing down all day. "Making trouble, as per usual," she said, before she shoved Tony over to me and did a runner.'

Danny stopped to wipe her eyes. She began haltingly: 'At about six, Tony started crying. Not just crying – screaming, high-pitched and pulling up her chubby little knees. And she was that hot.

'I skipped the bath and tried the bottle, but it was no good. So I rocked her, hoping she'd sleep it off. You never know with babies. But inside me I knew something was really wrong. At eight I rang the doctor's, even though I knew what Mum thinks of them, but there was only some machine and Tony was screaming so much I couldn't think straight.

'I stuck it another couple of hours and her screaming got less, but I didn't think she was better, just worn out. A funny colour too. She needed help badly. She needed her mum to take her to hospital.'

'That's what mums are for,' said Mab sympathetically and Ned nodded.

Danny took no notice, lost now in her story. 'All along it had been in the back of my mind to take her to Mum at the Red Lion.

'That's what I did in the end. Wrapped her up warm, put her in her pushchair and walked to the Lion. She'd stopped screaming altogether by now, which I still didn't think was a good sign.

'I s'pose it was ten or later. Now I think I should have got her to hospital myself . . .'

Danny stopped – stroked Sid for a few moments before starting again. Ned and Mab kept quiet.

'Anyway Phil came out first – I'd sent a message in for Mum. He was drunken angry. "What's all this?" he shouted and gave me a clout, although he looked round first to see no one was watching. "Can't a man get a moment's peace!"

'It was cold on the pavement and I was shivering hard. I'd forgotten my own coat, what with making sure Tony was warm. I think me looking so pale and weedy annoyed him more.

'"You're worse than your mum!" He gave me another sly bit of a slap.

'"It's Tony," I stuttered out. "She's sick. She's really sick."

'"That's it, is it? Sick. Sick my—! You just don't want to help . . ."

'He was about to smack me again when Mum came up, wearing a sparkling top, she was. "So what's this,

Danny? Haven't I told you never to bring Tony out? Not at this time of night."

'"She's real sick, Mum. I was frightened."

'As it happened, for once she wasn't too far gone to see just how worried I was. I think she was fed up with Phil's behaviour too.

'"OK, then. I'm tired anyway. Let's take her home and have a look."

'The trouble was that Phil came too, furious and arguing all the way, blaming me, Mum, poor little Tony. When we were in the house he was worse, lashing out at both of us so that I hardly dared take out Tony from the pushchair in case she caught it too. And Mum seemed to have forgot why we were there, trying to keep her end up with Phil.

'So I wheeled the pushchair into the front room and lifted Tony ever so gently and when I unwrapped her, she was pale as a ghost and sort of floppy. I felt more frightened than I've ever been in my life, so I yelled.

'I must have yelled loud because they both came running. And there I was holding Tony, tears running down my cheeks.

'"Oh my God. Oh my God!" Mum understood quick enough. She was pale as a ghost too. "Is she . . . ?" But she couldn't say the word. Nor could I. Phil didn't have a problem like that.

'"You've killed her now, have you?" he shouted at me, and went on from there, swearing and cursing, accusing me of all sorts of bad stuff.

'The moment Mum took hold of the baby, he got worse, battering me like he wanted to kill me – that's how I got these bruises and things. It's the ring on his finger what gave me the cuts. I was used to that. I just stood there. If I tried to hide, it only got worse. Besides, I was thinking of Tony. But then he started saying more things.

' "You think you're too young to be in trouble, don't you? But you're wrong. They've places to put away girls like you . . ." He went on with all sorts of things until he got on to "care" – how I'd be put into care because I was "out of control", how he and Mum would say how they couldn't manage.

'And that was true enough, of course, as I knew better than anybody, so I believed him about that. I knew I hadn't killed Tony – I loved her, I looked after her – but no one looked after me. They'd said things like that at school, talked of visits from social services and "care".

' "And your mum'll be happy to see you go," he carried on, "you've ruined her life, you know that, don't you?"

'I did know that. She'd told me so every day of my life. That was when I decided to go before they came to get me. And I thought I could find a phone box on the way and dial nine-nine-nine. Maybe Tony could be saved. Maybe she could be a medical miracle.

'So I went for a pee, but not really. Actually, I went upstairs, put on as many clothes on top of each other as I could – a coat would make them suspicious – and, before I could lose my nerve or Phil could lock me in, I was out of the door.'

Danny stopped, looked at Ned and Mab with red, swollen eyes. 'So that's how I got here. I hid in a lorry. Then I walked.'

She uncurled her legs from under her and stood up, as if to make herself braver. Sid landed heavily on the floor and swished her tail crossly. Danny didn't even notice. 'So you see why I can't go back.'

'You're safe here,' said Ned.

'I'll make some more tea,' said Mab.

'Told you it wasn't a nice story.' Danny sat down again as if she were exhausted.

Ned felt exhausted himself. He thought he would never feel sorry for himself again. He couldn't think of anything to say to Danny. She was sitting again with her head in her hands.

In a few minutes Mab brought through the tea and put it on a table. There were only two cups. She touched Danny on the shoulder. 'I've got to go.'

Danny was far too shattered to ask where Mab was going at this time of night. Or perhaps in her sort of life, a young girl leaving late at night wasn't so odd.

'We'll see you tomorrow evening?' Ned asked hopefully.

'I'm never far away.'

After the door had closed behind Mab, Ned took a cup to Danny. 'Drink up, then I'll show you your bed.'

Danny looked up at him. Her face was smudged

and swollen with tears and one of her cuts looked really nasty.

'You need some antiseptic.'

'Tomorrow.' She gave him a weak smile. 'Thanks though.' She sipped a bit at the tea, then looked up again. 'It helped. Talking. I don't know why. It doesn't change nothing.'

'At least you're not still outside in that cold smelly shed.'

'No . . . Won't your auntie mind? Me using her bed, I mean.'

'She's a very kind old lady,' replied Ned firmly.

12

The next morning, Ned woke early. He looked in at Danny but she was buried under the bedclothes. Now and again, he heard a faint snore. She had a lot of sleep to make up.

Accompanied by the ever-hungry Sidonie, Ned went into the kitchen, fed both of them and, when they'd finished, sat back at the table – this time with a piece of paper and a pencil.

There were just too many questions revolving round his head. Maybe if he wrote them down, he'd work out some answers, or at least be clearer about the questions.

Ned wrote carefully:

1. Is anyone looking for Danny?
2. If so, who?
3. What should she do?
4. Did the baby, Tony (Antoinette), really die?
5. Who is the old man with the beard?
6. Why did he want to question Danny?
7. How ill is Great-Aunt Ellen?

8. Will she come home again?
9. When will Mum and Dad come?
10. What should I say if Dad rings again?
11. How long will our food last?
12. Will Mab come back again?
13. Where can I find ointment for Danny's cuts?

All this took a lot of thinking and writing, and when Ned looked up again Danny was watching him from the door.

'Whatever are you up to? You're not at school now, you know.'

Ned decided not to argue. In fact he was glad she was being her usual difficult self – not like the evening before. 'Look for yourself.' He handed her the piece of paper.

She read slowly, then looked up with a grin. 'I can answer the last one. In the bathroom. Medicine's always kept in bathrooms.'

'There is a cupboard above the basin.'

'Told you.'

'You'd better look, then.'

Danny sat at the table. 'What I want is my breakfast.' She looked at Ned expectantly.

'I'm not your servant, am I?'

In the tussle that followed, with the cornflakes packet being snatched to and fro between them, the piece of paper with its important but unanswerable (save for one) questions, fluttered under the table where it lay forgotten.

But after breakfast – chocolate biscuits and

sandwiches – Ned remembered again and went up to the bathroom. The only trouble was, the cupboard was locked.

He found Danny standing in the little back garden, which was as far as she'd go out of the house. 'Cupboard's locked,' he said.

'Typical old lady. Afraid you'd drink poison and die.'

Ned looked at her face critically. The colours were even more violent by daylight. 'One cut's all red round the edges. Perhaps I should go to the chemist.'

'No you should not! Think of the nosey questions – "Where do you live, my dear?" And when you tell them, they'll be on to you. And me too. A sore cheek's nothing compared to what I've had to put up with.'

'A boy at school nearly died from an infected cut. Although he had come back from Africa.'

'I'm tougher than any stupid boy at your school! And I haven't come back from Africa.'

'The thing is I could buy a paper at the same time.' The idea had just come to Ned. 'See if there's any news.' He hesitated. He didn't want to upset Danny by mentioning her baby sister. But surely a dead baby and a disappeared sister would be news. At least in the local paper.

'What do you mean "news"?' asked Danny in the truculent tones Ned had begun to recognise she used when she was anxious. 'What's the news to us? We're lying low, aren't we?'

'Yes, I know.' Ned tried to think of a way to put things tactfully.

But Danny beat him to it. She turned away from him as she spoke. 'You're thinking we might find something out about Tony, aren't you?' Her voice quavered.

'Just possible,' agreed Ned, deciding not to mention that she might be news herself. 'It could be good news,' he added hopefully.

'You don't mind taking the risk?' She still had her back to him.

'It'll be fun.'

'Cheers. I won't forget this.' Her voice was muffled, as if she were trying to hold back her tears.

Not long afterwards, a heavily hooded figure left Lilac Cottage and started along the front.

The moment Danny had stopped waving from behind the lace curtains of the window, Ned pulled back the hood. Didn't the girl know that adults always suspect boys with their hoods up!

It was nice to be out. The sun glinted off the sea that was rolling over in pretty ripples. He didn't even bother to look when he passed the house where the old man lurked. This morning the world seemed a friendly, unthreatening place.

He turned away from the sea and towards the shops. He reminded himself he'd been there before with no problems. Sid hadn't followed him for once so there was no way anyone could identify him. He was just another boy, sent on an errand by his mum. That was it.

The chemist was further away than most of the

shops. Ned jangled his coins in his pocket in what he hoped was a casual way as he passed the newsagent – he'd buy the paper on the way back. Then, feeling a last toffee among the coins, he unwrapped it and popped it into his mouth.

The truth was, he was a little scared. There were more people around than on his last visit and more cars. Perhaps it was a Saturday. Ridiculous though it seemed, he'd really lost track of the day of the week. He thought it must be like this being a castaway on a desert island, and tried to make himself smile. But, after all, he wasn't on his own any more: he had Danny and Mab – well, some of the time.

Outside the chemist, he paused and looked up and down the street. Now he felt like an old-fashioned gunslinger before he entered the saloon bar and caused mayhem.

Then a man brushed past him and, following closely, he was in the shop too. He immediately wished he was anywhere but in the stuffy dark room. Then he thought of Danny's poor, battered face.

'Can I help you?'

Ned lingered at the back of the shop, while the man was served, then, the woman turned her attention to the boy.

She leaned over the counter and repeated louder, 'Can I help you, dear?'

Ned took a step forward reluctantly. Just his luck to find the woman from hell. Her head, peering towards him in the rather dim shop, seemed unnaturally large, with rolls of dyed blond hair springing above a round, reddish face with protuberant pale eyes, only half disguised by narrow glasses on the end of her snubby nose.

'I-I,' began Ned nervously. Now he would begin to stutter and flush too, probably. He must pull himself together. There was nothing illegal in buying antiseptic cream and his situation was no business of hers. He took three firmer steps forward. 'My mum sent me to buy some antiseptic cream for cuts.'

'Did she specify which one?' Her voice was very horrid: sharp and sibilant at the same time. 'Show me the cut, dear.'

'The strong sort,' he said. 'It's not me that's hurt, it's for my sister.'

'Is it, so.'

Ned noticed she sent out little flakes of spittle on her 's's. He retreated a little, but as he did so, she leaned even further forward so it looked as if she might tumble over and her huge head roll like a football at his feet.

Ned realised he was losing it. No more silly imaginings, just plain fact.

'She's five.' Lies actually.

'Is she, now.' The woman made no attempt to look along her shelves for the tube. 'Live locally, do you?'

'No,' said Ned quickly. 'We're from London.'

'Guessed as much. My sister lives in London. Walthamstow. Know it, do you?' There was something inquisitive and even threatening about her manner.

'No.' He didn't have to know everywhere in London. 'My mum wanted—'

Ignoring this, the woman carried on her train of thought. 'So you're up from London for the holidays. Not too cold for you?'

'No,' said Ned. 'Please could I—'

'Rented a house, I suppose. This time of year, there're plenty going. So which are you in?' Her icy eyes fixed on him and waited for an answer. This was feeling more and more like an interrogation.

'Rose Cottage,' answered Ned wildly.

'Rose Cottage, is it? No, I can't say I know it. Now Lilac Cottage I know, where that poor old Miss Fairley lived until they took her away . . .'

At this point, Ned had had enough. Either she gave him the cream or he ran for it before she accused him of – he didn't know what, but definitely something: perhaps attacking Great-Aunt Ellen.

'My mum's in a hurry.' He took his money out of his pocket to show he was serious. Grrh had passed over an envelope with money sent from his father, so he had no problems there. 'Can I have the cream please?'

'You Londoners. Always in a hurry.'

Ned refused to apologise. He felt as if he'd been in the shop for years. Besides, despite her grumbling, the woman was at last feeling about in a shelf he couldn't see below the counter.

'Fell over, did she, your little sister? Or did you push her? I know boys. Always up to something. Probably trying to hide it from your mum.'

'She fell. By herself!'

'Oh, yes.'

The lady re-emerged with a blue carton. 'How old is your sister, did you say?'

'Six.' Oh, no. Was she going to start again?

'Funny. I thought you said five before.' She gave him a suspicious stare.

'Nearly six.' Ned held out the money desperately. 'Six next Thursday.'

'Thursday, is it?' The spitting was getting worse but Ned held his ground. 'My sister in London has her birthday on a Thursday. Thursday's child is meek and mild. Is that right now . . . ?'

As the woman held up the carton as if to jog her memory, Ned contemplated flinging himself across the counter and snatching it from her hand. He was saved by the ringing of a bell at the door as a third person entered the shop behind him.

The odious woman's expression immediately changed to eager and attentive. Suddenly Ned was of no interest to her. 'Two pounds ninety-nine, and apply sparingly.'

She gave him his change and at long last he had the package.

Trying to look calm, he turned round for the door and only then realised that the man who'd just come in was a policeman.

The moment he was out of the shop, he couldn't stop himself running. He ran so fast that he ran straight by the newsagent, quite forgetting to pick up a newspaper. By the time he remembered, he had reached the sea front with the reassuring emptiness of the rolling sea and he couldn't possibly bring himself to go back.

One thing at a time, he told himself. He had the cream. Whatever the policeman's mission, he hadn't caught more than a glimpse of his, Ned's, face. Anyway no one was out looking for him – as far as he knew.

Taking a few deep breaths of good salty air, Ned slowed his pace to a relaxed saunter (well, a saunter, if not quite relaxed) and approached Lilac Cottage.

Before he'd time to get the key from his pocket, the door opened a few centimetres and Danny's frightened face peered out.

'Quick! Quick! Don't stand there like a block.' She grabbed his arm and pulled him inside.

'What's the matter?'

Danny slammed the door behind them, before whispering hoarsely, 'It's them. They've been here.'

'Who?' asked Ned, imagining all sorts of horrors.

Danny went in the living-room and slumped into a chair before answering. 'The police, you dumbo! Who else?'

13

Ned tried to think sensibly. 'You mean the police came in here?'

'Course not.' Danny sounded scornful, in the way Ned least liked. 'I wouldn't let them in, would I?'

'So they knocked?'

'Hammered, more like. It felt like the *blows of doom* on my head.'

'If you'd stop being so dramatic, I might understand what actually happened.' Ned felt exasperated. It was not as if he'd had an easy morning.

'As a matter of fact,' he said stiffly, 'there was a policeman in the chemist and I didn't get all hysterical.' Which overlooked his mad run home.

'They're not looking for *you*, are they? I'm wanted. There're gonna be police all over soon.' Danny jumped off her chair excitedly. 'I'd better get away now while there's time.'

'Sit down,' said Ned sternly. 'You're only making things worse, bobbing about. For all we know the policeman I saw was looking for a packet of aspirins, not you at all. Now what about your lot? How many were there?'

Danny sat down again, although reluctantly. 'I only saw one.'

'One! I thought there were hundreds, the way you were talking.'

'It only takes one, you know, and I'll be in prison for the rest of my life.'

'There's no point talking like that. Now tell me exactly what happened.' Ned recognised his voice sounded like his father's when he was trying to get information out of him. 'Incidentally,' he added, 'you haven't asked, but I did get the stuff for your cheek.'

'Cheers,' said Danny, without asking to have it.

'Come on then.' Ned sat down too. 'Let's have the story.'

'I was in the kitchen, doing a bit of cooking—'

'Cooking?' interrupted Ned, surprised.

'Well, I saw your aunt had a pocket of rice and Tony liked nothing better than a rice pudding . . .' Her voice trailed away.

'So what next?'

'Yes.' Danny rubbed her eyes. 'Next I heard this thundering and I looked through the window and saw it were the police. So I ran upstairs and hid.'

'That's all?'

'It's enough, isn't it!' Danny was indignant. 'You just don't know what it's like to be on the run and frightened all the time. At the very least, Phil'll bruise me up.'

Looking at her face, Ned resisted adding, 'What, more?' Instead he said, 'Sorry. So that's all you know?'

'When he'd gone I looked out of the upstairs window and I saw them – him – having a real go at that old tramp's door. Banged for ages, he did. Shouting he knew he was in there – the old man – and he'd have him out if he didn't come, whatever.'

'He went on for some time, did he?' Ned was thoughtful.

'I told you. Not that it had any effect. That old guy had more sense than to show a whisker to the likes of the police.'

'I'll tell you what,' Ned leaned back in his chair, 'I think that policeman wasn't interested in anyone in this house at all. He was after the old man and just hoped he might pick up a bit of info.'

'You think so? Honest?' Danny's face brightened remarkably. 'You don't reckon they were after me?'

'No, I don't.' Ned heard his father's sensible tones again. 'In fact, I'm sure not.'

'That's all right then.' Danny began to giggle. 'And I was about to leg it. And it was all the old nutter's problem, not mine.'

'That's what I think. But we'll know soon enough. They'll come back and chuck him out like they do squatters, as soon as they have the papers.'

'Heartless lot!' Suddenly Danny had her cross face back, although she didn't seem frightened any more.

Ned stared at her with surprise. 'You're not sorry for him now, are you? He's the one who grabbed you.

Remember? Terrified you witless. If I hadn't come, you might still be bound and gagged . . .'

'What are you like? I wasn't bound and gagged. How could I have eaten the chocolate fingers? I told you, he weren't so bad. We just got off on the wrong foot. Poor old guy. He's like me really, in hiding. Not doing anyone any harm neither in that empty house.'

'I give up! One minute you're scared for your life over nothing and the next you're weeping over a filthy old squatter who might have done you serious damage.'

'I never cry. I don't do your poncy weeping neither!' Danny flared up again so high that Ned regretted his own outburst. He must remember what a terrible time she'd been through and her dreadful situation.

'OK, OK. I'm sorry. The truth is I got a bit scared in town. What with the policeman and everything. There was a nosy old bag in the chemist too who kept asking questions.'

But this was a mistake too because Danny leaped up again. 'What do you mean, questions? What did you tell her?'

'I didn't tell her anything. Or rather I lied. I told her my mum had sent me. I said we came from London.'

'I s'pose that's all right then.' Danny sat down again.

'But the thing is,' continued Ned, 'I ran right past the newsagent so I didn't buy a newspaper, so we don't know any more about . . .' he paused, trying to work out a way of putting it tactfully '. . . how things are with your family.'

'Oh. Yeah.' Danny seemed deflated. She linked her

hands together and then unlinked them. 'I can't say I was choking to hear the news.'

'Sorry. I'll have another go tomorrow. I think we should stay put today, what with the police and everything.'

'Guess you're right.' After this they were both silent. The future didn't look rosy at all. In the end they went into the kitchen and ate an early lunch, including large portions of Danny's rice pudding – which had a remarkably cheering effect, so much so that they decided to investigate the living-room cupboards further. Danny found a skipping-rope; the rope was silky-white as if it had been hardly used, the handles were of shiny wood, inlaid with silver ball-bearings.

'I've always, always wanted a skipping-rope.' Her eyes were shining happily in a way Ned had never seen before. 'Mum thought it silly. Better to use your energy cleaning the bath, she'd say. And this is such a beautiful one. Do you think I can take it out into the garden?'

Ned was touched by her asking his permission. 'Aunt Ellen would love it to be used, I'm sure. Anyway it's probably Mab Angel's.'

As they walked towards the garden, Danny commented, 'She's a funny one, that Mab. Does she only come out at night? Like a werewolf or something?' She spoke quite casually but it gave Ned a start all the same. He really wasn't in the mood to explain Mab's peculiar story, even if he could.

'Sort of,' he said. 'Maybe she'll come later.'

He looked at her face. 'Hey, shall I get that cream for you?'

'In a mo.' Danny ran off with the skipping-rope, very inexpertly jumping and tangling her feet.

Ned walked to the end of the little garden where the lilac tree stood. He looked up at the white flowers – it was the white not the mauve sort – and sniffed their delicious scent. High above him, a couple of seagulls wheeled and squawked.

Then he looked back at the little cottage and saw the pantry window and the window to his aunt's room, where Danny had slept. The afternoon sun shone on the glass so it wasn't easy to see in.

'How about this?' cried Danny. She managed three jumps in a row before the rope coiled round her ankles again.

'You'll be a champion soon!' Ned shouted.

He didn't know what made him look up again and to the left, where the house stood next to Lilac Cottage. Probably it was the slight creaking noise as a window was eased open.

He stared curiously. He thought he could see a shadowy figure behind the pane. Then a missile came flying from the window, over the separating wall, and landed in a branch of the lilac tree. The window creaked down again and the shadow disappeared.

Danny was concentrating far too hard on her jumping to notice, so Ned went over to retrieve whatever had been thrown over.

It turned out to be a piece of lined exercise-paper

wrapped round a pebble from the beach. As Ned smoothed out the paper, he saw both sides were closely covered with writing.

He smoothed it out further and began to read the small, rather old-fashioned handwriting.

Dear Neighbours,
I am the old man who caught hold of the little girl (I believe she's called Danny). This was a very wrong and stupid thing to do for which I am sincerely sorry. Please forgive me and don't be frightened. My only interest is in the lady who lives in Lilac Cottage. Ellen Fairley. I saw her taken away a few nights ago and was so anxious for information that I grabbed Danny. I would never have hurt her. Now I have my own problem. The police have found me and will turn me out and who knows what else. They don't like squatters and they don't like odd behaviour, particularly from an old man with a white beard. I don't blame them. But they don't know my story. One day I'll tell it to you but it's too long for this bit of paper.

Ned paused to turn over the sheet.

The point is I've got to leave before they catch me. Now you see I'm going to trust you with my future because I know something about you. You're in hiding just like me. Don't worry, I won't tell on you. I'm sure you have your stories too – not as sad as mine, I hope.
I'll be gone by the time you read this. I'm heading right along the sea front in one of the little bathing-huts. There's a row of about a dozen and one is unlocked. If you hear any news about Ellen, good or bad, I beg you, let me know . . .

By now the writing had become so tiny and squeezed on the bottom of the page that Ned could hardly read it. The last line seemed to be something like:

I would go see Ellen myself, but how can I risk such a surprise after so long, when she's in hospital, too.

The signature was illegible, just a kind of scrawl.

Ned was about to show Danny the paper when it struck him that if he went fast enough, he might catch the old man before he left.

Dashing across the garden and causing a protesting 'Hey!' from Danny as he knocked the skipping-rope from her hand, he shot through the house to the front room and pulled back the lace curtain from the window.

He was just in time to see the old man striding energetically (not so decrepit, after all) past the window. Over his shoulders was a large backpack, and two plastic bags were in the hand that wasn't carrying his stick. Clearly, he was moving house.

Ned wanted to shout at him – nothing unfriendly, just to show he'd read the letter. But, since he didn't know his name, he was silent. In a moment the gaunt, hurrying figure was out of sight.

Ned stared for a moment at the sea, still a bright cheerful blue with curling white tips, and then let the curtain fall.

Really, the letter created more mysteries than it solved.

14

'Ned! What is it? What's the matter?' Danny was pulling at his sleeve. 'Is someone coming? Shall I hide?'

'No. No. It's not about you at all. Well, only incidentally.'

'What do you mean, "incidentally"?' Her voice was still filled with suspicion, or perhaps she didn't know what the word meant.

Ned, who hadn't planned to show Danny the letter until he'd read it again and had a better stab at understanding, realised nothing else would reassure her.

'Here.' He handed over the piece of paper. 'It was thrown into our garden from the house next door.'

Danny took the paper without asking any more questions and went over to one of the plump armchairs. The sun had dropped, making the room dim, so Ned turned on a frilly pink lamp before taking the other chair.

He watched Danny as she read. At last she folded up the piece of paper and handed it back to Ned. 'Told you so, didn't I?'

'What?'

'He was all right. It was a good thing he apologised though. You can't go grabbing people on the streets, whatever your reason.'

'That's what I think. It all seems a bit fishy to me. Why would the police want him if he's done nothing wrong?'

Danny gave a scornful cackle of laughter. 'The police want all sorts of people who've done nothing wrong. You just have to look different, that's enough for some of them.'

Ned, who'd always thought of the police as rather helpful and protective, felt on the defensive. 'He's not so innocent. He is – or was – squatting, you know.'

'Squatting,' exclaimed Danny, 'in an empty house! They should be happy he's there.'

'I don't know . . .'

'And as for innocence,' Danny continued self-righteously, 'I'm innocent, aren't I, and they're out looking for me. Am I right or am I right?'

'We don't exactly know,' began Ned tentatively, 'that they are looking for you. We think your mum or Phil will be out looking for you and will probably have reported you missing to the police, but that's not the same as saying you're guilty of something. After all—'

But Danny interrupted by jumping to her feet. 'Didn't you hear what I told you? Phil thinks I killed Tony. He thinks I'm a murderer!' Her voice rising on the last word, she burst into tears, ran out of the room and Ned heard her go up the stairs. Aunt Ellen's bedroom door slammed.

Ned sat where he was dejectedly. It would be no good following her for a bit. It was his fault for being so cowardly and not buying a newspaper. He looked at his watch: six o'clock. Too late tonight. If only they could discover Tony hadn't died, everything would seem brighter to Danny.

It was then that Ned had his idea. He wanted to run up to Danny at once, but he knew he should wait till she was calmer.

He felt restless, cooped up too long in the house, not even Sid to play with. Where was Sid? Ned got up and checked the pantry window in case it was shut. But it was wide open.

Perhaps he'd go out for a breath of air. The sun was low, casting a rich golden glow over the sea; there would be light enough for ages yet.

Making up his mind, Ned grabbed his jacket and went into the hallway.

'I'm going out for a walk!' he called up the stairs. As he'd expected, there was no answer. He opened the door and stepped out into the cool evening air.

Immediately his spirits rose. Carrying the burden of Danny's problems was a heavy weight. He reminded himself of his idea before turning right in the direction he'd seen the old man go. He hadn't been in that direction before which, in itself, cheered him.

The sea was quite far out, leaving a wide expanse of pebbles and occasional sand. Some of the pebbles were still damp, gleaming invitingly. He crossed the road and felt them roll under his feet. A swirl of seagulls rose ahead and, for a moment, the air was raucous with their cries.

They had obviously been feeding off something on the beach. He hoped it wasn't anything too disgusting. As he reached the spot, he saw crusts of bread and other stale food. The contents of the old man's bag, maybe.

Of course he was going to do a bit of a recce on him. Every walk needed an aim.

Ned continued along: sometimes head high, enjoying the fresh, salty air; sometimes eyes down as he spotted an interesting shell among the stones. Quite soon his pockets were filled with shells of all shapes and colours, including a chunky but miniature glass bottle – unfortunately without a message. He jangled them with his fingers in his pocket and liked the contrast of smooth and ridged, round and pointed.

Whistling a little under his breath, he began to think of his parents. Perhaps his father would ring again – although that would frighten Danny. Perhaps his mother had had the baby. He tried to imagine a baby in his mother's arms but quite failed. Girls are better at things like babies, he thought. Look at how Danny had looked after her sister. But he didn't want to bother about her just now. This was time off. He was enjoying being alone.

Soon a row of bathing-huts appeared, about a dozen of them, much smaller than the fishermen's sheds.

They sat on their own, well beyond the last cottage. Instead of being dark wood, they were painted pretty pastel colours, an odd sight in the middle of nowhere, only the vast sea in front and scrubland behind. Ned supposed that in the summer holidaymakers must spread all along the beach.

Now he'd arrived, he had to decide whether to turn round straight away or go further and run the risk of meeting the old man.

Just then, he saw a plume of smoke go up in front of one of the beach huts and then he saw the tall bent figure. The figure turned in his direction, paused, then raised an arm in welcome.

Should he do a runner? In the end, curiosity was too great and Ned advanced cautiously.

'So you came. I'm honoured. Are you hungry? Stupid questions. Boys are always hungry. At least I was when I was a boy. A long time ago, you may say.'

The old man was talking so much because he was nervous, Ned guessed. Odd to think someone like him could be nervous of a young boy. As the man spoke he prodded at his little fire, where six rashers of bacon had just begun to cook.

'I got your letter,' Ned offered.

'My apology. Deserved. Would you care for a chocolate finger? Your friend enjoyed them. She's a hungry one.'

'No, thanks.' Ned hesitated. 'I just wondered . . . You knew my great-aunt, you said?'

'Ellen . . . Your great-aunt?' He suddenly turned

away and began to prod even more vigorously at the fire.

'Careful,' warned Ned, 'or the bacon'll fall in.'

'Quite right. Quite right, young man.' He looked up again and there were tears in his eyes. 'You, her great-nephew. It's all a big shock. After so long. That's what I wanted to save her from: the shock.' Suddenly he put down his fork and advanced almost menacingly on Ned. 'Have you heard any news? Is that why you came? If you're her nephew, you must know how she is. She hasn't died, has she? That would be too cruel. Too cruel.' He stepped away again and began to shake his head, so his long beard swung backwards and forwards.

Ned thought it impossible that his clean, neat aunt could ever have known someone like this, however long ago, but he answered politely, 'I'm afraid I don't know anything really. But I don't think she's dead.' He pictured the grey face on the stretcher. 'Well, she wasn't when they wrote to me.'

'Wrote to you? Wrote to you! The hospital, you mean? What did they say?' He was on Ned again, his blue eyes rimmed with red, staring like a madman. Perhaps he *was* a madman.

Ned darted a glance behind him. Could he run for it, if things got bad? The old man's legs were long, if spindly. He began to regret approaching him. And yet there was something pathetic about him, heartfelt.

'They said she'd had a stroke. I should have visited her but I couldn't.' He paused. 'Like you guessed, I'm in hiding too.' Now he'd trusted him.

'Yes. Yes. I couldn't visit her because she might not welcome me. I was watching her, you see. I didn't want to frighten her. She's old too now.' The man fell back into some kind of depressed meditation.

'Your bacon's burning,' pointed out Ned.

'Yes. Yes. You're a good boy. No surprise, being her nephew.' He pulled off the bacon on to a piece of newspaper. 'Tell me, are you descended from that sister of hers, Mab? She was a bright little girl.'

'Oh, no!' Ned was shocked. 'Mab drowned!'

'Drowned? Drowned.' The old man began muttering and seemed so distressed that Ned thought it best not to tell him the whole story. Anyway it was far too complicated to explain how Mab was back again, quite likely in Lilac Cottage at this very moment.

'Won't the police get you here?' he asked, to change the subject.

'No. Not here. I shouldn't have been in that house. Down here, they won't worry me. Besides this is Ellen's bathing-hut. Hasn't she ever brought you down here?'

'No. Look, I have to go. Danny'll be worried. But I'll find out about Aunt Ellen for you – somehow. I've decided to go to the hospital. I want to find out too.'

'And you'll let me know?' The urgent mad look was in his eyes again and his beard began to waggle.

'I promise.' Ned turned to go and then turned back. 'I don't know if you plan to see my aunt but, if so, maybe you should cut off your beard. It's just not Aunt Ellen, if you know what I mean.'

Startled, the old man fingered his beard. 'I've lived

on my own so long . . .' He was mumbling again and Ned felt sorry for him.

'I could bring some scissors and cut it off quite easily.'

'You could?' The old man seemed dazed.

'Oh, yes. Anyway I'll report back and let's hope it's good news.'

'Please God, good news.'

The last Ned saw of the old man before he began to run home was his thin arms stretched to the sky, as if in prayer.

15

'I'm back! Danny! I'm here!' Ned called as soon as he entered the house, worried that Danny would think he'd deserted her.

A quiet voice came from the living-room. 'We're in here.'

Ned turned the knob and went in. There were Danny and Mab sitting side by side on one of the big armchairs, arms round each other's waists. At their feet, Sid lay stretched out like a furry black rug. He couldn't help smiling at the contrast in what they wore: one World-War-II-1945-little-girl-neat, the other unisex-2006-casual-bagginess.

'Do you know what an odd sight you are together!' he exclaimed.

'Mab says that, in her day,' Danny grinned up at him, 'girls dressed quite differently from boys and they didn't play rough games neither, unless they were "tomboys" who liked to pretend they were boys. Funny word, isn't it, "tomboy" – as if you said "marygirl".' She laughed at her own joke.

'At least you've put on that antiseptic stuff.' Danny's face now had thick patches of white cream as well as everything else. 'Aren't either of you interested in where I've been?' he asked. Really, they were a bit too cosily 'girls together' for his taste. In his experience, when girls started behaving like that they soon started to make fun of any unlucky boy who happened to be within distance.

'Where *did* you go?' asked Mab. She looked interested at least.

'I followed the old man to the beach huts.' Ned tried not to sound as if he were boasting.

'You did too!' Danny was as impressed as he could wish. 'I just told Mab about his funny letter. Did you talk to him?'

Ned turned the chair round from the little desk and sat down so he was facing the two girls. He felt a bit important, which was a nice, unusual feeling. 'He was cooking his dinner on a fire he'd made on the beach.'

'What was he cooking?' asked Danny eagerly.

'Bacon,' answered Ned briefly. 'That's not the point. The thing is, it's Great-Aunt Ellen he's after.' He saw Mab sit up straighter and grasped all of a sudden that whatever was the reason for the man's visit to Seaburgh, it almost certainly concerned Mab more than any of them. He wondered if she'd told her story yet to Danny. 'He wants to see her, but he doesn't want to frighten her by popping up all of a sudden. I told him he'd be a lot less frightening if he cut off his beard—'

'I like beards!' interrupted Danny.

'Not if they're dirty and tangly,' began Ned, but then he noticed the intent expression on Mab's face.

'Who is he?' asked Mab into the silence.

'Yes,' echoed Danny. 'Who is he? Did you ask him?'

Ned thought. The truth was, he hadn't exactly asked him. He remembered something else. 'He asked about you, Mab.'

'What do you mean? You told him about me?'

'No. No. He seemed to know you from the past . . .' Ned stuttered to a stop. Mab's past was an awfully long time ago. 'He said you were a nice kid.'

Mab's face grew more thoughtful but she didn't try to provide any explanations. 'You say he wants to see Ellen?'

'I promised to go to the hospital tomorrow.'

Both girls stared at him. Eventually Danny said, 'But how can you, without being found out – and then where will they take you?' She didn't add, 'And what about me?' But Ned could hear it in her voice.

'Actually, it's not just that I felt sorry for the old man, although I did, but here we are living in Aunt Ellen's house, eating her food, sleeping in her beds, and yet we haven't even bothered to find out just how ill she is. It's just not very grateful!' Ned stopped abruptly, embarrassed and rather red in the face.

'You're right,' said Mab. But Danny turned away.

'There's another thing.' Ned tried to make Danny look at him. 'This morning I decided to ring your mother. I'll tell her you're OK and ask about Tony. Isn't that just brilliant? No newspaper. Real info. All I need is a telephone number.'

'What's he saying?' Danny looked as if she couldn't believe her ears and needed Mab to explain.

'It's a good idea,' said Ned defensively but he could see he should have been a lot more tactful. He might have been, if they hadn't seemed so 'girls together'. 'Obviously I can't do anything without you saying yes.'

Danny still seemed puzzled, nearer tears than anger. 'You want to ring my mum?'

'She'll be worried, after all. Whatever Phil said or did, she's still your mum.'

'I don't believe this!' Danny still appealed to Mab. 'He said he'd never tell nobody I was here and now he comes out and says he's going to ring my mum. How's that for cheek? And he tells *me* what *my* mum'll be feeling. You know what her last words to me were? "You're not my daughter. I never wanted you. You've made my life a misery from the moment you were born." She said that, plus a few choice words I won't use in front of you nice people. Don't you see? She doesn't care where I am! As long as I'm not anywhere near her. Now do you understand?'

At this, Danny did burst into tears. Mab had kept quiet during her speech. Now she put her arm round her, and Sid stopped looking like a rug, stretched, and went over to the door.

Ned thought he'd like to be let out too. He'd handled it badly, but what was Danny saying? She's hiding because she expected to be chased, but now she says her mother wouldn't look for her.

'Sorry,' he said.

There was a pause. Danny's tears ran silently down her face.

'Ned was trying to think of a way to get news of Tony,' said Mab eventually.

Danny's tears speeded up.

'Sorry,' said Ned again. 'I won't ring if you don't want me to.' He decided not to add that he couldn't anyway without the telephone number, because it sounded too unsympathetically sensible for Danny's emotional state. He thought it really was true that girls cried more than boys − even strong, brave girls like Danny, he added to himself more kindly.

'In my day,' said Mab, 'all sorts of terrible things were happening all the time. In the war, that was. People dying, people disappearing. The worst thing was not knowing: not knowing if someone you knew and loved was under that heap of rubble at the end of the street; not knowing if your father would ever come back from the war, or even where he was. We really longed for news more than anything. Knowing the truth, even if bad, made us feel more in control.'

Danny had stopped crying and was listening to Mab. Not for the first time, Ned thought how much older Mab seemed than either of them, even though her real life had stopped at about their age.

'You mean I might feel better if I know about Tony?'

111

Danny's voice was hardly above a whisper. '*Whatever's* happened.'

'Yes,' answered Mab.

'But we were going to look in the newspapers.'

'Ringing your mum is quicker.'

'I'm not going back there whatever!'

'No. No. Of course not.' Ned and Mab spoke together.

'Go on, do it!' Danny surprised both of them by jumping off the chair. 'Do it now!' She reeled off a number far too quickly for Ned to remember. 'Just say Danny's fine and she wants to know about Tony. Just that. Nothing more!'

16

Danny's sudden change took Ned by surprise. He felt nervous and unprepared. He began to mumble about doing it from a call box so they couldn't be traced, and then suggested they should get something to eat first.

But Danny stood in the middle of the room shouting out the number.

In the end Ned was driven to stuttering, 'I – I can't do it while you're here. Write down the number.'

'One minute you're so keen and the next—' began Danny, before Mab took pity.

'Let him do it on his own, Danny. I'll come with you to the kitchen and teach you how to make roly-poly pudding with no eggs and no sugar.'

Danny stopped in mid-shout. 'That was wartime, was it? No eggs, no sugar. I don't know how you did it.'

'My mother was good at things like that.'

'Your mother?' asked Danny.

'Yes, I'll tell you about her while we're cooking. Now write down the number for Ned.'

Obediently, Danny wrote down the number and went out with Mab.

Without thinking more, Ned sat by the big old telephone and dialled. The ringing tone seemed extra-loud and old-fashioned too. Then there was a voice.

'Yes?' It was a gruff man's voice. Not young, not even middle-aged. Ned was confused.

'I'm sorry. I—'

'Who is this?'

'It's nobody . . . I mean—'

'This is . . .' the man said a long number very fast. 'Who do you want?'

Despite his muddle, Ned realised he'd dialled a wrong number. 'I'm sorry . . .'

'Wasting people's time!' The man slammed down the phone.

Danny's head appeared round the door. Mab was just behind, failing to restrain her.

'I heard you speaking!' cried Danny.

'Wrong number,' muttered Ned.

'Wrong number!' Danny's mouth and eyes were round. 'I didn't give you no wrong number.'

'I dialled it wrong. Sorry.'

'Come on, Danny,' intervened Mab. 'Give him a chance.'

Danny allowed herself to be led away.

Ned picked up the heavy receiver again. He dialled carefully. This time it rang a long time before a sleepy woman's voice answered.

'Hello?'

'Is that Danny's mum?' Ned suddenly remembered he didn't know her name.

There was a short pause, a stifled gasp, then the woman's voice came again, quite different this time. 'Danny, is that you?' It was almost a scream. 'You don't know the worry you've caused me. Half the police force are looking for you. I'm out of my mind with worry—'

Ned interrupted. 'It's not Danny. It's a friend. She says to tell you she's fine. She wants to know about Tony. She's very worried about Tony.'

'Worried about Tony! What about me? I haven't slept a wink since she left. Between her and the hospital—'

'The hospital?' interrupted Ned, clutching at straws. 'Who's in hospital?'

'What?' The woman was taken by surprise. 'My Tony, that's who's in hospital. Poor little mite. She's a fighter, though. Doing all right now, they say.' She stopped abruptly. 'What's it to you? Who are you? I want to speak to Danny!' She was increasingly agitated. 'You've done something to her! What've you done?'

'N-no!' Ned needed to make her listen. With an effort, he controlled his stutter. 'She's here. She's safe. But she doesn't want to speak to you because of what you did to her! You and your Phil. She's scared!'

He stopped and heard a little hiccough and something that might have been a sob from the other end.

'Danny just wants to know about Tony,' said Ned, more calmly. 'She'll be in touch when she wants to.' He jammed down the phone. His hands were damp and shaking. He wondered if Danny's mother had guessed he was a child.

The door burst open. This time Mab wasn't trying to stop Danny. 'She heard most of what you said.' Mab raised her eyes resignedly.

'Who says I'll ever go back!' screamed Danny. 'Who gave you a right—'

'Oh, shut up,' said Ned, surprising himself and the others. 'Do you want to know about your baby sister or not?'

Danny's face crumpled. She plonked herself down on a chair. 'Yes. Please.' Her voice was very small.

'News is good,' said Ned in what he now thought of as his grown-up voice. 'She's in hospital. Definitely not . . .' He decided not to say the word 'dead'. 'Your mum said she's a fighter and doing all right, so the hospital say.'

'Oh. Oh,' murmured Danny. Ned hoped she wasn't going to cry again. Instead she surprised him with a smile. 'Thank you. Oh, thank you.' She paused. 'Sorry I yelled at you.'

'Not to worry,' Ned mumbled embarrassedly. Luckily, just as he could feel a blush rising, Mab got to her feet.

'Come on, Danny. We were cooking, you know.'

'I'm starving,' agreed Ned heartily. 'I hope we're not just having powdered eggs. They sound disgusting.'

As Mab and Danny went to the kitchen, Ned took a breath of relief. One decisive action taken successfully, even if Danny did consider herself still on the

116

run. Then he thought: but tomorrow I've promised the old man to visit Aunt Ellen in the hospital. His relief ebbed away.

A second later the telephone rang. Ned jumped away from it. Was it the police? They'd tracked his call. He'd talked too long. Now Danny would never smile at him again.

The phone rang and rang. Ned looked at it, terrified.

'Well, you can't just let it go on for ever.' Mab had come in quietly. 'Danny's halfway out of the window anyway. Might as well know the worst. As I told you before, any news is better than no news.'

'They won't give up,' muttered Ned. The bell seemed as loud and threatening as a siren.

'Go on,' encouraged Mab.

'You do it, if you're so keen.'

'I can't. I'm not really here, am I? They wouldn't hear my voice.'

'I suppose if it is the police,' said Ned, 'they know where we are anyway.'

'I dare you,' said Mab.

Ned picked up the receiver. His hand was trembling. 'Hello.'

'Ned! Great news! Your mother's had the baby! You've got a beautiful baby sister. It's a miracle! We've waited ten years for this . . .'

Ned's father's voice came and went over the airwaves, sometimes loud, sometimes soft, as if his huge excitement was distorting the sound.

Ned tried to take it in. He got the point, of course,

117

but he couldn't really feel it was much to do with him. His dad seemed so far away and kept talking without waiting for Ned to say anything. Eventually, he did stop, although the airwaves still vibrated.

'Tell Mum I'm glad,' said Ned tentatively. His conversation with Danny's mum had seemed more real.

'You're all right, Ned?' His father paused in his celebrations. 'You sound a bit odd.'

'It's the line,' said Ned.

'Can I speak to Aunt Ellen?'

Why hadn't he a lie ready? 'She's just gone out.'

But his dad was much too exhilarated to worry. 'Tell her the news. And it won't be so long before we're back.'

After Ned put down the receiver, he turned away from Mab's curious face. 'Your mum's had a baby, has she?'

But he wouldn't answer her. It all seemed too remote. He was making his own life without any help from his parents, and they shouldn't expect him to suddenly switch into theirs.

Tomorrow he had to go to the hospital and find out about Aunt Ellen, and there was the old man on the beach, and that was without thinking about Danny's problem. What did a new baby somewhere the other side of the world matter compared to that?

'Let's eat,' said Ned. 'I'm starving.'

17

Mab wasn't there when Ned set out to find Great-Aunt Ellen the next morning. Of course she wasn't, Ned told himself, she was never around in the day. Yet his aunt was her beloved sister – well, half-sister anyway. She had to have most interest in the outcome of his investigations – apart from the old man.

The truth was that ever since Danny had appeared, she'd switched her attentions so that Ned hardly felt she cared about him. Perhaps she went where she was most needed. Or perhaps she was becoming more shadowy, like ghosts do. That was funny – thinking he knew how ghosts behave.

It was a dreary morning, the sky a sullen grey with little wind. It would be just his luck if it were cooking up for another storm. Ned increased his pace, avoided looking at the heavy sea, and began to whistle.

Danny had been very quiet over breakfast. He'd considered reminding her of the good news that her baby sister was alive. No one could accuse her of being a murderer now. But her expression had seemed too fixed in anxiety for him to try any cheering words.

At least she'd run to the door as he was leaving and thrust a packet of toffees at him. 'I found them in a tin in the larder,' she'd said, before adding, 'I hope you noticed my cut's nearly healed.'

So she wanted to give him some credit. Ned felt in his pocket for the nice sweet bulk of the toffees. His fingers also felt the letter from the hospital. It was because of the letter and a map that had come with it that Ned knew where to go.

Ned stopped and decided to take one more look. He had to take a 415 bus from the main street, which would carry him to the biggest town in the area – about a two-hour journey, he reckoned.

He'd pulled out the paper and was studying it (for the tenth time) when he heard steps approaching. He looked up.

'Oh, you!'

The old man came closer with the quick stride which had surprised him before in one so ancient and gaunt-looking. He wasn't even using his stick. There was something else different about him.

'Are you going to the hospital?' he asked as soon as he was close enough for Ned to hear.

'You've cut half your beard off!' cried Ned.

'Yes. Yes.' The old man was impatient. 'I only had a penknife. But that's not important. Are you going to see her?'

'If I can.'

120

'And that's where she is!' The old man snatched the letter. His gnarled hands quivered as he held it close to his blue eyes, rimmed with red and half covered by thick white eyebrows. They needed a cut as much as his beard – although, to be honest, the jagged job he'd done hadn't much smartened his appearance. He really was very odd: so tall and bowed and thin, with large grey trainers, baggy jeans and a black jacket with 'Whiz Kid' written on the back. Where had he got that? He just looked like a crazy old tramp and, if he, Ned, didn't want to draw attention to himself, he should get away from him as quickly as possible.

'I've got to go,' said Ned, attempting to grab back the paper.

'All right. In good time. I don't like the look of this . . .' He was reading and muttering, mostly to himself. 'No. No. Not good. "A stroke . . . unable to talk or even write . . ." Poor Ellen. And myself so near at hand . . .'

'Please,' said Ned.

The old man seemed to make up his mind. 'A bus journey, that's all.' He handed back the letter. 'Good luck, young man.'

'Thanks. I'll let you know of course.'

'Yes. Yes.' He was back to impatient mode. 'You do just that.'

Ned hurried off. The meeting had upset him. Who was the old man really? There were too many mysteries since he'd arrived at Lilac Cottage.

* * *

121

The bus (which was more like a coach, bright green with a red stripe) was out of Seaburgh and speeding through the countryside in a matter of minutes. Ned had been lucky. He'd just finished reading the timetable at the stop – which informed him the number 415 only came once an hour – when this bus appeared, stopped for a moment to pick up himself and one old woman, before speeding off again.

Ned sat near the front, the woman near the back; between them, rows of empty seats. Sitting quietly, sucking one toffee after another, Ned felt almost relaxed – despite his mission. When the driver turned on a radio above his head, he felt quite holidaylike, even though the choice of music seemed fixed in the distant past.

'*We'll meet again, don't know where, don't know when . . .*' sang along the driver.

He wasn't even too worried about finding out where the hospital was. When he'd bought his ticket, the driver had told him, 'It's not far from the bus station. Stay on to the end, lad.'

So there he sat, half listening to the weird songs – '*We're going to hang out the washing on the Siegfried Line . . .*' – half watching the wide flat fields change places one with another. Now and again, the pointed grey spire of a village church broke the monotony. Ned thought they looked like rockets ready to shoot off into the sullen sky. Well, at least it wasn't raining.

He must have fallen into a half-doze because their entry into the bus station took him by surprise.

Suddenly he was under a roof, with all the noisy reverberations of coaches moving in and out and people queuing, climbing in, climbing out, hurrying about their business.

'Turn left out the station,' directed the driver as Ned stumbled out of the door and down the steps. 'If you turn right you'll end at the docks; next thing, you'll find yourself packed in a container ship to China.' He laughed heartily at his own joke.

Ned hadn't taken in he was coming to quite such a big and busy city. Till the driver made his joke, he hadn't even taken in that it was a port. But once on the streets, he could smell the closeness of the sea, feel the energy in the people who dashed past him: one solitary boy not quite sure where he was or where he was going.

He pulled himself together. The driver had told him to turn right, so that was easy enough. Ahead was a wide road, decorated with large signs: 'Felixstowe', 'Ipswich', 'Harwich', and filled not just with cars and vans but huge lorries, loaded with crates that must have come up from the docks.

He walked steadily. Soon the massing grey clouds bunched over the town and cold thin rain began to fall. It was hard not to think longingly of the cosy warmth of Lilac Cottage. To spur himself forward, he pictured his aunt's grey face on the stretcher that first night. It can't have been much fun for her either, arriving sick and helpless in this hard city.

Glancing down side streets, Ned saw rows of small

red-brick houses with a few glass-fronted shops. There was not a flower to be seen, nor a tree. He pulled up his hood against the increasing rain.

It was half an hour, but it felt like hours, before Ned saw a vast sign saying 'HOSPITAL' and pointing to a modern glass-and-concrete building. Then there were other signs: 'CASUALTY', 'OUTPATIENTS', 'IN-PATIENTS'. It was all very muddling. For a second, Ned wondered whether his mother had had her baby, his sister, in a hospital like this. But the whole idea was too remote to consider.

'Where's the reception, please?'

The man he'd asked, a hurrying young man in a white coat, looked at him curiously but then a bleeper sounded at his waistband and he pointed – 'Left, right, right, left' – before hurrying on his way.

Ned followed his instructions and eventually joined a queue at a long desk. Two women, often on the telephone, tried to answer queries. They used brisk, loud voices and, like everyone else in the city, seemed in a hurry.

At least he had time to prepare his question: 'I've come to visit my Great-Aunt Ellen Fairley. Please could you tell me where she is?'

The woman – straight black hair and blood-red lipstick – didn't seem to understand him. 'What do you say?'

'I'm looking for Miss Ellen Fairley. She came in a few days ago. By ambulance.'

'Did she now?' the woman continued, unconvinced.

She called to her colleague, 'This little lad's looking for a great-aunt. Any takers?' Then she turned back to Ned. 'Where's your mum – or dad, if it comes to that?'

Ned had been on his own or with Mab or Danny for so many days that he was genuinely surprised by the way the woman was talking down to him, as if he was an inferior species. He'd quite forgotten that adults think children incapable of having any sensible life on their own. But if he wanted to get his way, he'd have to play up to it.

'She's gone shopping,' he said.

'Gone shopping, is it? Look, sonny, I don't know what you want here but slip off now like a good boy and let us get on with our work. Yes, sir?' She turned to the man behind Ned in the queue.

Reluctantly, he gave way and moved back a little way to regroup. Perhaps a toffee would help. The moment he stuck his hand in the pocket he realised his mistake: he should have shown the hospital's letter.

Resigned to the funny looks he was getting (he was dripping wet apart from anything else), he took the letter in one hand and joined the queue again.

'You, again! I thought I told you to scarper.' The woman was even nastier than before.

Ned plonked the letter on the desk. 'Please read this.'

She glanced down. 'I see.' Her expression was no kinder. 'So this aunt does exist. But you still can't go in.'

'Why? I've come all this way—'

A finger with a pointed red nail waggled in his

face. 'One, you are an unaccompanied child. Unaccompanied children are strictly forbidden on the wards. Two, it's now twelve-thirty and visiting hours aren't till three-thirty. So scarper!'

This time Ned did give up. He wound his way back through the corridors until he was once more at the front of the building. It was pouring with rain, he was very hungry, and he had utterly failed.

'Hey! Ned!' A hoarse whisper came from somewhere hidden to his left. Then a low whistle.

Ned peered round the corner. He caught sight of a tall shape. 'You! What are you doing here?'

He found he was actually pleased to see him.

18

'I couldn't wait, could I?' The old man had a plastic bag over his head and another over his shoulders. 'Have you seen her? How is she?'

'Let's find somewhere out of the wet,' suggested Ned. Perhaps then he'd take off the bags and look a little less odd.

'But how is she?' The old man spat as he spoke and Ned noticed that his teeth looked as if they might pop out too.

'I didn't see her.'

'You didn't see her! Is she – is she all right?'

'I don't know. They wouldn't let me in.'

The old man looked as if he might collapse. 'Not see her,' he muttered. 'Yes. We'll sit down somewhere. We'll rethink.'

'There's a café I saw down a side road.' Ned had noticed it because it looked so battered and fugged up with steam. The kind of place where the old man wouldn't stick out too much, anyway.

* * *

In another five minutes they'd settled into the café, which turned out to be surprisingly comfortable inside. The old man consented to have his layers of plastic removed, and Ned ordered tea and a Coke and two plates of bacon, egg, sausage, tomatoes, baked beans and chips. There was no point in starving, however difficult things were.

'I *will* get to see her,' said the old man. 'Nobody will stop me.'

Ned looked at him over a forkful of beans. He looked at his wild hair, his weird clothes. Then he looked at his bright eyes, his set mouth and his hawk nose. He saw that nobody *would* stop him – and that gave him an idea.

'I want you to do something for me after lunch,' he said. 'And if you do, I think we can get in the hospital together.'

'I'm all yours,' agreed the old man, 'until visiting hours.'

'One more thing,' continued Ned.

'Well, now that's asking. Fire ahead.'

'What's your name?'

It was the first time Ned had seen the old man smile, let alone laugh. His whole face changed, the lines of anxiety displaced by smooth planes. Ned saw that hundreds of years ago he must have been a good-looking man.

'Doug,' he said, putting out his gnarled hand. 'Pleased to meet you.'

The name might have rung more of a bell with Ned

if he hadn't had his mouth stuffed with eggs and bacon. As it was, he just noted that was a name he'd heard recently, and carried on eating. After all, they didn't have that much time to carry out his master plan.

Even though Doug had promised to obey Ned after lunch, it was a real problem to get him into the shop.

'I haven't been in one of these places for decades.' He went into muttering mode and pulled on his beard.

'You promised!' Ned tugged on his arm.

Luckily, there were no other customers inside to gawp at this strange couple entering the barber's shop: the young boy and the tramp-like old man. At last Ned got him into the chair. 'Short back and sides,' he said, imitating a film from the past.

'You want me to take this lot off!' The barber, an old man himself, exclaimed in horror.

'That's right,' agreed Ned cheerfully.

'But I'd have to wash it first!' His face looked even more woeful.

'I guess that's true enough.' Doug was staring at himself in the mirror. 'I wasn't aware I'd let myself go so far.'

'I could wash it,' volunteered Ned, adding, 'maybe you can cut off some first so as not to waste shampoo.'

In the end that's what they did. The barber, bribed with double his normal charge (Ned hoped the money his parents had put in the envelope wouldn't run out) went into a back room and emerged with a pair of shears, with which he did a first cut. Then he and Ned washed the rest before he got down to a proper shaping and serious shave.

'Oh take the beard off altogether,' said Doug. 'Ellen only ever saw me clean-shaven.'

The final result was startling. Even the reluctant barber looked pleased with himself. The handsome man that Ned had caught a glimpse of earlier had reappeared. He was old, of course, but fine-featured and sympathetic-looking. Why ever had he allowed himself to get into such a state, Ned wondered. But that was for another time. He looked at his watch.

'We've got to get moving!'

Doug was staring into the mirror, standing up now. 'Hold on there, young man. I don't quite like the look of the rest of me. Tell me, sir,' he addressed the barber, with whom they were now on friendly terms, 'is there a clothes store in the area?'

'Two streets up: W & W Snape & Sons. Just what you need. Not over-reliant on modern fashions.' The barber smiled, obviously proud that he'd started this Cinderella transformation.

'Right you are. Snape & Sons. Excellent.'

'But, Doug,' objected Ned, 'we've no time and no money.'

'We've enough time and enough money.' Doug sounded quite steely. 'How much do I owe you, sir?'

To Ned and the barber's equal surprise, Doug produced a large brown envelope filled with banknotes.

'He's not a bank robber is he?' whispered the barber in an aside to Ned, but the idea was too absurd.

'He's a man of mystery,' was all Ned could offer.

Next thing, he'd paid and was out of the shop, striding along with Ned racing behind. It had stopped raining and a sharp blue was slicing up the clouds.

W & W Snape & Sons turned out to be just what the barber described: not reliant on modern fashions. It must have been there for centuries, thought Ned. But Doug was satisfied. In ten minutes flat he'd allowed an aged gentleman, in a dark suit (perhaps W senior) to fit him with a pair of brown corduroy trousers, a blue shirt and a tweed jacket.

'Your trainers, sir?' hinted Snape. 'I fear we don't stock shoes.'

'No time,' said Doug.

'The older customer has begun to favour the softer shoe,' advised Snape consolingly.

'Quite,' agreed Doug. 'How much do I owe you?' And once more the envelope was produced. But this time W Snape senior was far too discreet to show any reaction.

'It's been a pleasure to do business with you, sir.' He bowed them ceremoniously out of the shop.

'And you, sir.'

Doug began striding again, but found time to point out to Ned the value of good manners.

Ned was silenced. He pictured the wild threatening creature who had got hold of Danny. Now he was more like a country gentleman.

They reached the hospital on the dot of three-

131

fifteen. To Ned's dismay, the same black-haired witch was on reception, but this time she hardly glanced at him.

'Miss Ellen Fairley. Nelson ward. Floor six, lift eight.'

'That's good,' muttered Doug as they set off, 'not intensive care . . .'

Ned guessed his muttering reflected anxiety. 'Perhaps we should take some flowers,' he suggested, to give him something specific to worry about.

'Good thinking.' Doug looked round wildly.

'You go on up,' said Ned. 'I'll find some.'

'No! No!' Doug was suddenly frantic. 'Certainly not! No!' He gripped Ned's arm. 'I'm coming with you. We'll see how the land lies.'

So they forgot the flowers and started up the stairs. Ned had pointed out the lifts but Doug said he'd rather walk.

'Six floors!' exclaimed Ned, thinking he'd probably have a heart attack before they reached the top.

'Slow and steady, slow and steady.'

It took them fifteen minutes, with many rests, to make the sixth floor. Doug leaned on Ned, panting. Eventually he whispered, 'You go on. I'll just get my breath back.'

'They won't let me in without you,' pointed out Ned.

'OK, OK. I'll show myself to the nurses.'

Doug wanted to see his old friend, Ellen, so much that it had reduced him to a trembling bag of nerves.

'I expect that'll be fine.'

So when they got to the nurses' station Ned announced his grandfather needed a rest, and the nurse, who was kind and motherly, found him a chair in a little room off the corridor. 'I'll follow you in a moment,' he said to Ned as the nurse bustled off.

Ned walked into the ward slowly. He wasn't so confident himself. He wasn't even sure he'd recognise Great-Aunt Ellen. Luckily, there were plenty of other visitors so no one took any notice of him.

'Ned? Ned, dear.' A hesitant voice was repeating his name from near the window.

Ned looked and saw an old lady in a blue knitted bed-jacket watching him.

'Aunt Ellen! Oh, I *am* glad you're better!' He was beside her in a minute, surprised by how pleased and unembarrassed he was to see her. The point was she was such a very kind old lady and smiled so happily to see him.

She patted the bed beside her. 'I've been very worried about you. The hospital sent a letter, didn't they? And someone's looking after you?'

Lies again, thought Ned. Well, he couldn't duck this one. 'Yes,' he said firmly, and after all, Mab was looking after him.

'Good. Good. You see, I'm not quite better. I've got my speech back. But my arms and legs aren't working quite the way I'd like. That's why I'm still here.' She smiled gently. 'I'm improving daily, that's the important thing.'

As she began to ask him about the cottage, Ned's

attention wandered. He was facing down the ward, where any minute he expected Doug to appear. Should he warn Aunt Ellen that an old friend was coming? He remembered Doug had been worried about shocking her. At least he *looked* all right now but perhaps someone from the past was always a shock. Perhaps it would be such a shock she'd have another stroke.

Ned wished he knew more of Doug's story. Again he had a slight sense that he'd heard the name recently. 'Do you have many visitors?' he asked.

'Oh, no. It's too far for my friends from Seaburgh. Besides, I'm supposed to keep quiet. You're my treat.'

Ned was becoming increasingly worried in every way. He was worried about Doug's arrival and worried about his non-arrival. He'd had plenty of time to rest.

'I need the toilet,' he told his aunt. 'I'll be back in a moment.'

It didn't take very long to discover that Doug had vanished. No sign of him in the little room or by the nurses' station or in the toilets or anywhere else. He'd disappeared into thin air.

19

'You haven't seen an old man anywhere?' Ned asked a couple of passing nurses. But they were all too busy to stop and only gave him a quick blank stare.

So he went back to Great-Aunt Ellen. He noticed at once that she looked paler and her voice was less strong. Her white freckled hands pulled at the sheets.

'Did you say the baby was born, dear? My memory's not so good. I expect you told me.'

'Oh, yes!' Ned was glad to make things seem normal. 'A lovely girl.' He didn't know where the 'lovely' came from but it sounded right.

'A lovely girl,' repeated his aunt in a weak yet contented voice. 'So you'll all be going home soon.'

Ned thought about this. The 'all' presumably referred to his family, as if they were in Lilac Cottage with him. Of course Aunt Ellen would never guess he was there on his own. 'Not quite yet,' he said, noticing that her eyes were beginning to close.

'I'd so like to see the baby,' she murmured, before closing her eyes altogether.

At that moment a large nurse appeared and gave Ned a grim look. 'I hope you're not tiring the poor lady.'

Ned smiled weakly and the nurse bent over to put her fingers on Aunt Ellen's frail wrist, while keeping her eyes on the watch pinned to her vast bosom.

'Is she all right?' asked Ned anxiously.

'Fine. Dozing.'

'I'll be off then.'

'So you should,' said the nurse, giving the impression it would have been better if he'd not come in the first place.

Ned walked away from the hospital feeling that this was one of the longest days of his life. He also felt lonely. Doug's disappearance really depressed him. After all the effort and expense they'd gone to to make him presentable, it was actually annoying as well as depressing. Cowardly, too.

Ned looked round the busy pavements without much hope of seeing the gaunt bent figure. Yet he couldn't have gone far. Best thing was to get back to the bus station and head for home. Probably Doug would pop up somewhere on the line. Was he really missing a weird old man who lived in a beach hut?

But at the bus station, he discovered there was only one more bus to Seaburgh that day and it didn't leave for two hours. He stood uncertainly at the exit. The sun was still shining, although sinking fast. Perhaps he'd turn left instead of right and head for the docks and the sea.

Apart from his visits to Lilac Cottage, Ned knew nothing about the sea nor the ships that sailed from one country to another. When his parents travelled abroad, they took aeroplanes. Twice he'd gone with them, to Italy and Spain, and when he'd looked down, he'd seen, far below, shimmering blue water. But it had hardly seemed real, just as the black dots or stripes he could just pick out hadn't seemed like real boats.

So he was quite unprepared for the scene at the docks. A continual stream of container ships was approaching, taking their turn for the cranes to unload their packaged cargo. They were led in by tugs, small but strong motor boats. There were huge open ships, loaded with great lengths of iron or steel. Further out to sea, gigantic tankers, whose oil came in through underground pipes, sat almost on the horizon, like black ten-storey buildings.

A ferry, raised up on stilts out of the water, came whooshing towards a different part of the port. In another second it settled down and, wallowing like a huge duck, made its way for the last hundred metres or so.

The smell of salty sea was very strong and above his head a large gathering of gulls wheeled noisily. None of the busy, shouting men took any notice of a single boy, so he became braver and went closer. Almost at the dockside, he spotted a notice: 'PUBLIC VIEWING POINT'. This sounded like a good idea. He turned right and followed a path which wound upwards, eventually reaching a series of stone steps ending, as far as he could make out, in a concrete platform surrounded by an iron rail.

He arrived at the top, puffing a little, and saw that there was already one other person with the same idea. He was leaning on the rail, as if tired, and staring out to sea. Even though he had his back to him, he was easy enough to recognise.

'Doug!'

Doug turned round slowly. 'Well, Ned. Yes, here I am. I guess you're mad at me.'

For the first time, Ned understood what was odd about the old man's accent: it had the drawling sound of an American. There'd been so much stuff going on around him that he'd never had time to listen properly. But it was calm up here above the sea. The setting sun, turning golden, reflected in the water and the energy and noise of the unloading tankers was distanced.

'I'm not cross,' he said, not quite truthfully. It was strange having an old man treat him so seriously. 'Surprised. I couldn't think where you'd gone after all the trouble we'd taken to smarten you up.'

Doug turned back to the railing. 'You have a point there, young man.'

Ned came and stood at his side. 'It was a bit cowardly, if you want the truth.'

'Cowardly?' Doug kept his eyes on the sea. 'Not far off. But there are mitigating circumstances.'

'What?'

'Maybe I'll tell you my story and you'll understand better.' He turned to face Ned.

With the glow of the setting sun warming his smooth shaven face, Ned couldn't help thinking how extraordinarily different he seemed from the crazy old tramp squatting in the house next door to Lilac Cottage.

'If I had an old friend turn up, I'd be glad to see him. That's all I think.'

Now Doug became more agitated. 'She was all right then? Could she speak? Did she know you?'

'She knew me immediately and, yes, she could speak. She was just weak, her arms and legs not too strong.'

'I could be her arms and legs,' began the old man eagerly, and then stopped and sighed heavily. 'That was how it went wrong. One reason, any road. I lost a foot in the war.'

'You lost a *foot* in the war!' exclaimed Ned, quite amazed. He stared down at Doug's long thin legs, which ended in perfectly normal – if extremely battered – trainers. Or so it seemed.

'Didn't mean to shock you. Things like that happen. It was all a very, very long time ago. I can scarcely remember what it felt like to have two feet.' He gave a smile as if to cheer Ned up. 'Think of it this way. When folk tell me to put my best foot forward, I don't have to worry over making the choice.'

'I'm sorry,' said Ned, looking down at his own feet, which seemed to be twitching rather inside their trainers. He couldn't help wondering what alternative object was inside one of Doug's.

'Hey, shouldn't you be catching the bus to Seaburgh, not standing here humouring an old man?'

'There isn't one for' – Ned looked at his watch – 'over an hour and a half, and I want to hear your story, I really do. And if it's about Aunt Ellen's past, then I probably know more than you think. It makes it almost my *right* too, as her great-nephew,' he added firmly.

Doug smiled. 'How old are you?'

'That's not the point.'

'Well, I warn you, it's not a happy story. Not like one of those computer games where you can win.'

'All the stories I've heard since I came here have been sad. It doesn't mean they can't have happy endings.' He could feel the obstinate expression on his face – what his dad called his 'iron mule look' – but he really did want to understand Doug's mystery.

'I can't tell a story standing up.' Doug moved to the back of the platform where there was a stone bench fixed to the floor.

Ned guessed that his speedy but uneven gait must be due to his foot – or lack of it. He followed Doug and they sat down side by side.

20

'At the start,' said Doug, 'there's the happy bit. Even though there was a war on, we were happier than I've ever been before or since.'

Ned saw he was going to have to ask questions if he was to get a clear picture. 'Who are "we"?' he asked. 'And what war?'

'Ellen and myself, of course. World War II.' Doug seemed surprised.

Ned wondered if he was being stupid. Already the story was finding echoes in his memory. It was just that too many new things had been happening to him in the last few days.

'I was a pilot, a bomber pilot, brought over from the US to finish off the war in Europe. My squadron was based on this coast. Each night we flew out over this very ocean.' Doug paused and stared ahead, as if he were picturing the great black bombers taking off across the waters. 'Our job was to smash the German spirit by smashing the German cities. We certainly did the latter. Night after night.'

He paused again, as if imagining for real things Ned had only seen in films: burning cities lighting up the night sky, aeroplanes spiralling downward in a cascade of silver bullets.

'Then I met Ellen.' His old man's hoarse voice changed to a dreamier note. 'You young chaps don't know what love was like then. Wartime made us all romantics, you see. We knew each night-raid might be our last. When we said goodbye, we said it as if we might never come back. Which is not to say we didn't have fun. You wouldn't credit it now, but I was the best dancer on the base and Ellen, although she wasn't the show-off type, she could swing on my arm as light as a feather. And pretty! She was the prettiest girl I'd ever seen, with a skin like a rose petal.'

Ned began to feel a bit uncomfortable at this point. I mean, next thing he'd describe what it was like *kissing*! After all, this was his Great-Aunt Ellen, not some starlet or something. He listened as Doug described his walks with Ellen along the dykes, besides fields planted with corn and cabbages. Then he was on to Lilac Cottage and playing games with Ellen's little sister. And, suddenly, very late in the day, Ned realised he did know this story.

It was part of the story Mab had told him on that first stormy night when they'd sat in bed together, one at each end. Doug – the old man – was the airman who'd been shot down and never returned. Then Aunt Ellen had tried to kill herself and Mab had drowned saving her.

'I know about you!' Ned interrupted excitedly. 'You're the American airman who died!

So how could he be alive? Sitting on this bench, telling the story from his point of view? He wasn't another ghost, was he? 'How come you're here?'

Doug stared at Ned and then leaned forward and put his head in his hands. There was a long silence while Ned idly watched a ferry plough its way out of the harbour rise on its stilts and turn right for the open sea. Had he offended Doug?

Eventually, the old man lifted his head. He spoke slowly and deliberately. 'I was shot down on the night of December sixteenth, nineteen-hundred-and-forty-four. I crash-landed somewhere in Germany. My foot got jammed in the wreckage. Some German soldiers got me out. I became a POW, a prisoner of war. I lost my foot and part of my leg. A German surgeon amputated it after gangrene set in. But I lost more than that. I lost my memory. My mind was a blank up to the moment I found myself in the camp. The doctors found it quite amusing. They used to say I must have done something worse than terrible that I didn't want to remember. And this was at a time when truly terrible things were taking place. I became scared they were right. I just about lost my wits too.'

He looked up and tried a half-hearted smile at Ned. 'Not many laughs, eh? Shall I proceed?'

'Of course. You can't stop now.' Ned was indignant.

'OK. So then the war ended. The allies freed us prisoners from the camps. But what were the authorities to do with me? They could give me a new foot, but they couldn't give me a new memory. Of course, they could tell I was American by my accent. They even thought they could work out roughly what US state I came from. So in the end they sent me to a war veterans' hospital in Kentucky. That's south-west America. I spent quite a few years there just surviving. But, understandably, they got fed up with feeding me. After all I was perfectly healthy, a big strong man, even if I was a count short in the limb section.'

'Didn't anyone know who you were?' asked Ned. He couldn't imagine anyone being so alone.

'They tried quite hard to find relations – with posters and TV too once that took a hold of the country. But nobody seemed to know me – or want a disabled man who'd lost his marbles, it comes to the same thing. I got myself a trailer with my veteran's pension and got myself a job too, working with horses. There're plenty of horses in Kentucky. It's a beautiful place. I was solitary all right but I wouldn't call myself unhappy. Just out of keeping with the rest of the world.

'I had my horses, though. Not for riding, you understand; for looking after and talking to. A big stud farm, it was: two hundred horses, brood mares, foals. What a sight when they turned them out on the spring-green meadows! They jumped about like a bee had bit them. I loved watching those creatures.'

The old man stopped and looked at Ned. 'I guess I'm boring you, rambling on.'

'No you're not.'

'Good. That's good. You're a nice boy. So things went on like that. Quiet. Even. My boss was getting old like me but we didn't really notice it. He valued me, paid me properly. I put it in the bank mostly, since I had nothing to spend it on.'

Ned thought he understood now about the roll of banknotes Doug had produced in the barber and the men's outfitters.

'My boss was old, as old as me,' continued Doug, 'and one day he died. Tipped over at the races after a big win. Fine for him. Not so fine for me. I'd never reckoned much on his son but, to do him justice, he kept me on, although I was good for nothing more than pottering by then. It was the fellows he mixed with that were the problem. They'd put back a six-pack or two, then come down to the stables and challenge each other to back the wildest horse they could find. Not that any horse is wild if it's treated right. I used to try and stop them. These horses were worth thousands – even hundreds of thousands – of dollars, aside from anything else. So they didn't like me. No sir. Called me all sorts of names.'

Doug darted a quick look at Ned. 'Not for your ears, young man. Well, the words I could take. Why should I care? But one evening, not so long ago, maybe a year back, they started on what's wrongly called "horse-play". Horses don't play like idiot men do.

'They started telling me I should ride. Why didn't I get up and show I was a man instead of hanging around the place spoiling their fun? The young boss knew perfectly well about my foot – he'd known since he was in short pants – but he'd drunk too much to think straight.

'So they threw me on this horse and whacked his backside till the poor beast took off at a gallop. I lasted for a while, hanging round his neck, but I knew I'd be off soon and, as it turned out, I shot off just where there was a wall – and that's the last thing I knew for a while.'

He stopped as if reviewing the moment.

'What happened next?' asked Ned impatiently.

'I woke in hospital. I'd broken my collarbone, cracked several ribs and had a serious bump on my head. Not too bad, all things considered. I was glad to think with all the blood from my head, those boys thought they'd killed me. Terrified of me dying and terrified I'd sue them if I recovered. But I wasn't interested in them because while I was in hospital, something strange began to happen. I'd get these odd flashes, like pictures on the TV. One, in particular, kept recurring. A pretty young woman.'

'Aunt Ellen,' breathed Ned.

Doug nodded. 'I'd just about given up thinking I'd ever get my memory back. It was over half a century ago since I'd known who I was. I had a new life, even if it wasn't too great just at the moment. In fact, I guess I almost didn't want to be disturbed. But there was no avoiding that face.

'After a bit I told the doctors, and I became quite a celebrity: the war-hero who got shot down and lost his memory, and fell off a horse and found it again. I was in the papers all over again, and soon I could remember everything: my home town, which was no great shakes – I'd been glad to go to war; my parents, who were both dead decades ago; no brothers nor sisters, a few cousins who didn't interest me nor me them. Nothing much in my past, except for one person – your Great-Aunt Ellen.

'You may wonder,' Doug turned to Ned, 'why in all those years I hadn't set my heart on another woman. There was the odd time it seemed halfway possible but you have to remember I was a cripple who'd lost his memory, an odd-ball loner who lived in a trailer in the woods and took more note of four-legged animals than any human.

'But after Ellen came back to me, I truly believed I'd been waiting for her all this time. Of course I wasn't fool enough to believe she'd been waiting for me.

'I was so restless with all this in my head, I didn't know what to do with myself. I couldn't go to the stables any more and I began to hate my trailer. So one day I upped and left. Locked the door and left.

'I went into town, drew most of my money out of the bank – they were surprised, I can tell you – and hopped on a Greyhound bus for the nearest big city where there was an international airport. Had a bit of a problem there. No passport. So I was there in a little room for days, weeks. That was the worst.

'But it didn't change my mind: I was determined to see Ellen before I died. I didn't think too hard whether

147

she was still alive, married, widowed. I just put all my energies into getting to her. Or to where I'd last seen her, just about sixty years ago.'

'And then when you got there, she was carried off in an ambulance,' nudged Ned as Doug fell silent.

He looked up. The sun had dropped nearly below the horizon and his ruddy complexion was dimming with the pallor of evening.

'I'd been there a few days,' murmured Doug. 'Just watching her. Seeing what was what. It wasn't hard to spot she lived on her own. I hadn't been so happy for years, just being near her. I felt just the same for her as I had those long years ago.'

'If you'd spoken to her then,' pointed out Ned, 'we wouldn't be in the muddle we're in now.' He glanced at his watch. He didn't mean to be hard-hearted but if Doug had any chance of going back to the hospital *and* catching the last bus, he'd have to speed things up a bit.

'I'm scared,' said Doug simply. 'I was scared before she was taken away and I'm scared now.'

'Why? I don't see . . .'

'No,' Doug sighed. 'You don't know about dreams.'

Ned thought this wasn't quite true but he let it pass.

'What if she doesn't remember me, if I meant nothing to her? I couldn't bear that. I'd rather keep my dreams and not try for the reality.'

Ned couldn't think of anything to say to that.

'I made her suffer so much. And what did you say, her sister drowned because of me?'

'It wasn't your fault,' said Ned weakly. He couldn't go into Mab's story now. Not if they were going to catch the bus. 'If you're not going back to the hospital,' he said, 'then we should get to the bus station.'

'Yes. Yes.' The old man seemed very tired. 'It's been a long day. I'll just sit here a moment. You go ahead. Danny will be looking out for you.'

'I could give you a hand.'

'No. No. Keep a place for me. But don't worry. I just need a moment alone.'

By now Ned really was worried about missing the bus, so he left the old man sitting staring into space and hurried off the viewing point and away from the sea.

He ran, in fact, so keen was he to get to the bus station. The exercise, after sitting still for such a long time, made him feel hot and flushed. As he dashed about looking for the right number bus he glimpsed a large face on a poster.

He might have stopped, but at that moment he spotted his bus and the driver was in his seat, revving up the engine. He leaped on quickly, grabbed a seat and only then looked out of the window to search for the poster.

Just as he'd thought: Danny's face. Above it was printed the word: 'MISSING'.

He had no time to read more, as the bus sped away.

21

As usual, Ned was glad to be welcomed back to Lilac Cottage by Mab Angel.

'Danny was in such a state, I had to come,' she told Ned straightaway. 'I've been teaching her card games to calm her down.'

Ned tried and failed to picture Danny calmly laying down a deck of cards. 'I've had quite a day,' he began. Then he remembered how deeply everything concerned Mab and stopped. He didn't feel up to telling her immediately. 'Where's Danny now?'

'She's making jelly in the kitchen.'

Ned could see that Mab was longing to ask questions. It seemed odd that a ghost didn't know everything automatically, like God or something. Perhaps it was because her appearances in the world were so limited: only in Lilac Cottage trying to comfort someone.

'I will tell you all about it. Just give me something to eat. I'm starving.' Seeing Mab disguising her disappointment, he relented enough to add, 'Great-Aunt Ellen's recovering fine. She talked to me quite a bit before she got tired. But the stroke's still affecting her legs, and one arm, I think.' Ned recalled his aunt, lying frail and pretty in bed. 'I certainly got the feeling she's planning to come out soon.'

'Then she'll need a lot of looking after,' said Mab in an anxious kind of way.

'I suppose so.' Ned found himself suddenly picturing the newly elegant figure of Doug. If only he didn't have so many hang-ups. 'If I don't eat soon, I'll die,' he cried, starting in the direction of the kitchen. And, as he went, he couldn't help thinking that it was quite strange to talk of dying to someone who's dead already.

Danny and Mab and Ned sat round the kitchen table. Ned had already eaten a whole bowl of spaghetti and was gobbling down Danny's jelly. It was a very lurid colour, half lime-green and half orange, and Danny was exceedingly proud of it.

'Next time, we'll do it in three parts,' said Mab, 'with a pink milk jelly at the bottom.'

Ned looked wonderingly at the two girls. There was something odd going on here. Since he'd returned, Danny hadn't asked him one question about his day. He'd given her openings a couple of times, but she'd looked away and started talking about making ice-cream.

He had been going to tell her about the 'MISSING' poster in the bus station – surely she needed to be warned they were seriously searching for her – but now

151

he was beginning to think she didn't want to know about anything outside the here and now in Lilac Cottage.

He'd heard the word 'trauma' used for people who'd been through terrible experiences and just couldn't cope any more. Perhaps that was where she was at now.

So he said nothing, and when they went through to the living-room, Mab got out Prince's Quest.

It was hard to concentrate. Beyond the windows he thought he could hear the waves higher than usual. After a while Sid pushed open the door and came purring across the room to where they sat on the floor. Her fur stood up and felt damp and cool. She'd obviously just come in. Ned thought of Doug and wondered where he was, whether he'd somehow managed to get back to Aunt Ellen's beach hut – with that wad of money he could afford to take a taxi even – or whether he'd stayed in town and maybe even visited Ellen, his long-lost love.

In a minute, he'd tell Doug's story. After all, it had nothing to do with Danny's problems, and anyway she'd always been surprisingly nice about him. Perhaps she thought they were two of a kind: both outsiders. He, Ned, never felt like an outsider, even though he was living such a weird life. He supposed he'd never really doubted his parents would come back when it suited them. Doug and Danny were living on the edge in a quite different way.

'Your turn, Ned. Or are you asleep?' Danny's impatient voice cut into his thoughts.

Ned took his knight off the board with a decisive gesture. 'I want to tell you about meeting Aunt Ellen today, and Doug too.'

'Doug? Who's Doug?' asked Danny nervously. Ned had forgotten she didn't know the old man's name. Then he saw Mab's eye fixed on him.

'Doug was the name of Ellen's boyfriend,' she said slowly. 'He was killed on a bombing raid over Germany in World War II.'

'No, he wasn't,' said Ned.

Now both Mab and Danny took their knights off the board.

'Doug's the old man with the beard, although he hasn't got a beard any more. He came to the hospital too. I met him there. He wanted to see Aunt Ellen. But first I got him all cleaned up, beard right off and new posh clothes.' He tried not to look too proud about this but it was fun to see the amazement on Mab and Danny's faces. 'Later we met down by the docks . . .'

As Ned retold Doug's story – about the prisoner-of-war camp, the amputated foot, his lost memory, his going back to America, his life looking after horses and the dramatic return of his memory – he realised just how extraordinary it was. Mab's enthralled face told him. Doug was a man who'd loved a woman he hadn't seen for sixty years.

'So was there a full handkerchief-and-tears reunion?' asked Danny as he finished. Clearly she found it hard to believe in romance for people quite so old and decrepit.

'Well – no, actually. He didn't dare face her.' Ned could see this was a bit of a let-down.

'Crap happy ending,' commented Danny, confirming his view of her attitude.

But Mab was silent and thoughtful.

'Thank you, Ned,' she said eventually. She turned to Danny. 'Doug *will* go to see Ellen. It's just taking him a little time. You don't have to rush things after so long.'

'I don't know about that.' Danny was as argumentative as ever. 'In their position, I'd think getting on with it was the most important thing. After all, she might pop off at any time.'

Mab smiled. 'So might we all.'

Ned suddenly knew – it was something in Mab's smile – that she'd told Danny her story while he was out.

'I think Doug will go and see Ellen,' he said. 'Mab's right. It's not like some silly soap. They can't just jump into each other's arms.'

'With her in bed and him with one leg, they'd be hard put to jump anywhere,' said Danny, smiling cheerfully.

For a moment Ned almost hated her. Then he thought, Danny had nothing but her cross mother and the dreadful-sounding Phil to go by, so a story of true love would hardly hit the spot. Even he could see his parents quite loved each other – a bit too much sometimes.

'The thing is,' he said, 'I've no idea where Doug is now.'

'Oh we don't have to be responsible for *him*!'

Although Danny's tone was aggressive as ever, Ned saw she was quite right. It would be mad to worry about an old man who'd managed all his life on his own.

'He'll be all right,' agreed Mab.

Ned glanced at Danny. Sid had jumped on to her lap and both of them had a sleepy, contented look. He certainly wasn't going to tell her about the 'MISSING' poster tonight. Was it possible that Phil wasn't so bad and that Danny's mum really loved her daughter? No, that couldn't be true. At least not about Phil. Danny's descriptions had been too vivid, too real. Besides, the bruises on her face were there still, evidence that just couldn't be imagined away.

'I'm going,' said Mab quietly. Clearly she had noticed Danny's eyes closing and planned to slip away.

'You usually do.' Ned knew he sounded bitter. Probably it was just exhaustion. But who was it always got the help round here? Not him, certainly. Yet it was he who'd spent the day trying to sort out problems and Danny who'd stayed at home playing stupid games with Mab.

He felt a light touch on his arm. 'Don't think like that,' whispered Mab. 'Be pleased with what you've achieved.'

Then she was gone. If she'd stayed, Ned might have told her how lonely he sometimes felt. How he wished his parents were more *there*. This holiday was nothing special. Ever since he was school age, they'd been dumping him with various people in various places. Of course they didn't bash him up, they even loved him, but it didn't make his life *easy*.

'Ned.' Danny had opened her eyes again.

'Yeah.'

'From what you said, the docks and everything, it sounds like you went to my town. Where I lived till I ran away,' she added, as if he might not understand.

'Didn't I tell you the name before I went?' Ned's mind immediately conjured up the face on the poster. Although he'd recognised it as Danny, it hadn't really been like her: the girl in the photograph had neat hair, a smooth, unbattered face and a big smile. She was wearing school uniform. He still wasn't going to tell her about it – not tonight.

'If you did say the name, I didn't want to know.'

'No. Well.'

'It's just that I was thinking –' she paused and stroked Sid as if to give her courage – 'I was thinking that if Mum said Tony, my sister Tony,' she looked at Ned as if to make sure he'd got the point, 'is in hospital, that's where she'd be, in the same hospital as your Great-Aunt Ellen.'

'I suppose she might—' began Ned, but Danny cut him short.

'And I was thinking more that I'd go to visit her.'

'What!' Ned didn't think he'd heard right. 'But you're terrified of being found. You hardly dare leave the house.'

'I love her, see.' First taking Sid in her arms, Danny

got up, and cat and girl stood over Ned where he crouched in one of the chairs. Two sets of greenish eyes stared down unblinking. 'If I see she's all right, I won't care about anything they can do to me.'

22

The night was long and restless for Ned. He could hear the waves outside, not as if there was a storm, but churning away just like all the thoughts going through his mind. Danny's bright face in the photo, mixed with her poor battered one now. Doug as an old tramp with unkempt and filthy clothes, mixed with the smart old fellow who'd told his story. Aunt Ellen, lying so fragile and weak in bed, came to life again as a pretty young woman with red lipstick and high heels. Even Mab, who'd returned from death to help him, changed from a neat little girl in a pleated skirt to a wild mermaid sinking under the waves.

But it was when Sid turned into a huge black polar bear with glassy eyes and growling toothy mouth that Ned cracked.

'I'm out of this now!' Still half asleep, he leaped out of bed and began to pull on his jeans and sweatshirt.

As his eyes opened a bit further, he noticed, to his surprise, that there was already some light coming through the thin curtains. He pushed them aside and saw that it was a grey day. Everything was grey, in fact: sea, sky and the whole landscape. The waves were thick and rolling heavily one after the other, breaking with hardly a splash. A gust of wind blew the curtains into his face. Pushing them aside, he could see a few seagulls: they were grey too. All in all it was a desolate, forbidding sort of day. The sort of day you had to take action or go under.

Ned knocked on Danny's door and then opened it. 'I'm off!' he announced to the humped backs of Danny and Sid. Neither stirred. So he shut the door again and bounded down the stairs. Stopping only long enough to grab a handful of biscuits from the larder (if he didn't eat he wouldn't grow, and he didn't want to be the smallest in the class for ever), he dived out into the cool morning.

How cool, he wasn't aware until he'd gone several paces along the front. A brisk wind was blowing from the sea and the all-grey look to the day had developed an unhealthy yellow tinge to it. Perhaps it was just the sun trying to force itself up over the horizon but it somehow felt more threatening, like the start of a sci-fi movie when a gang of little green men are targeting the world for an out-of-space visit.

He stuffed a couple of biscuits into his mouth and took a step backwards as a larger wave than usual broke violently, throwing high spray in his direction. The tide was already higher than he'd ever seen it. Only a thin rim of the beach remained, the pebbles rolled against each other by the force of the waves. They made an angry, grumbling sound as if they were fed up with the disturbance.

Soon all the houses were left behind and he was walking through the scratchy scrubland. He was going, of course, to check out Doug. The high sea must be awfully close to his little beach hut. But perhaps he wasn't there. Perhaps he'd checked into a posh hotel in town and even now was sitting beside Great-Aunt Ellen's bed in hospital. Ned imagined him holding her small age-spotted hand while he told her his story.

A gust of wind flung up spray from another extra-large wave. Or maybe they'd all become extra-large. He took a few more paces inland and strode out faster.

Five minutes later, he stopped and looked round. The row of houses was very small now, left far behind, and yet he still couldn't see the group of beach huts. Had he walked so far last time? He didn't think so.

Although he was several metres from the edge of the sea, something in the water caught his attention. It was a smooth patch; he saw one and then several more. Curious, he moved closer.

Above his head, a group of seagulls was gathering. They were quite high in the sky but suddenly, without warning, one swooped down, as if as curious as he was.

'Here! Mind out!' he shouted out and shielded his face. But they weren't interested in him.

Now he could see what was flattening the water: long planks of wood were riding the waves, whooshing in as if they might land on the beach, and then being drawn out again.

Something's broken up, thought Ned. A ship, presumably. Then one of the planks floated in close to him, like a narrow surf board on the crest of the wave, and he recognised where it came from. It was the colour, wet though the wood was, that gave it away: pink. The pink of Lilac Cottage and the pink of Great-Aunt Ellen's beach hut. It must have been washed right away and broken up.

Now he could see other coloured planks and he realised that the whole row of half a dozen little huts had vanished. He moved closer to the water. Had Doug been inside when Aunt Ellen's hut had been swept away?

'Be careful, young man!'

Ned turned round to see where the voice had come from. At precisely that moment a larger wave than all the others rode in from far out to sea. The first thing Ned knew was the breath knocked out of his body, as something that felt like a steamroller bowled him over and then rolled him round, round and round like a ball. He didn't even feel the weight of water crashing over his head. He just felt as if he'd lost all control and was as helpless as one of those grumbling pebbles he'd spotted earlier. In fact they were rolling round with him, all mixed up with sand and shells.

Then they began to be sucked from under him as the tide drew the wave out again. If he wasn't careful he'd be drawn out with them into the murderous sea.

Dimly, above the watery roaring in his ears, he heard a voice.

'Take hold of the stick, Ned! Ned do you hear me?'

Up till then, Ned had kept his eyes tight shut, but now he forced them open. The salt and sand stung horribly, but near his left eye a stick appeared, waggled, as if battling with the current, and then disappeared again. Now he felt the will to struggle. He wasn't going to be bundled out to sea like a pebble! Even if he did feel bruised all over and had a terrible pain in his chest. Obviously he couldn't stay under water for many more seconds. Flailing his arms, Ned tried desperately to get above the waves.

For a moment he thought he'd succeeded. His eyes and nose were out, and he'd just time to spit out some salty sea and take a breath of air before he was knocked down again. He'd also seen Doug. He was shouting from the edge of the water, holding out his walking-stick.

Ned understood: he must get hold of it and Doug would pull him in, although he doubted the old man was actually strong enough. If he went into the water, he'd be knocked over in a moment. It wasn't just that he was old but he also had only one good leg.

The stick appeared again, water rushing by it, forcing it away from him. Ned grabbed for it wildly. To his surprise, he got hold, and almost at once he felt a strong pull to the beach.

Less than a second later, he found himself in shallower waves and then hardly in the sea at all. For several minutes he was too busy getting water out of his mouth and air into his lungs to think of anything else.

He sensed, however, the tall figure of Doug standing over him.

Eventually, he lifted his head and gasped out, 'Thanks.'

'I don't know about that.' The old man leaned forward to give him a hand up. 'If I hadn't called out, maybe you would have seen the wave before it hit you.' He watched as Ned stood upright, water streaming from every part of him. 'I suggest we move quite a lot further up the beach.'

Ned staggered after him obediently. He felt battered all over, as if someone had been whacking him with a cricket bat. Also freezing cold.

Several metres up, they came to the flicker of a small fire and a pile of clothes and cooking things. Ned stared dazedly.

'A series of big waves came up just before dawn,' Doug spoke almost casually. 'I was in the hut. Luckily, I don't sleep well any more. The water was like a huge animal licking at the door. Then there was a great roaring. I was out in two seconds flat. Next minute the hut was reduced to matchsticks. The whole row, in fact. I expect you spotted the floating planks. If I hadn't fallen into a doze I'd have stopped you before you got anywhere near the water.' He took Ned's arm. 'Here, sit on this rug. Once you can walk, we'll get you home to a hot bath.'

Ned sat down thankfully. He could hardly take in

what Doug was saying. There had been more big waves earlier? He shook his head to clear the water from his head.

Doug put a blackened can on the fire and produced a tea bag from his pocket. 'I reckon we're landlubbers, that's what we are. No respect for the sea. No understanding. Well, I learned my lesson and I guess you've learned yours.'

'It was terrifying,' whispered Ned. He noticed his hands were shaking.

'I've lived inland all my life. I know about fields and woods, even mountains, although I'm no expert. The ocean just never came into my life. The only thing I can think, it's like the wildest stallion in the world.'

Ned was recovering enough to think that a horse would never be as strong as the power he'd felt as he was churning round under the waves. 'I was only a metre or two from the shore,' he muttered. 'But the sea wanted to take hold of me and force me into deep water. I'd never have come back.' He shivered violently. He couldn't help thinking that's exactly what had happened to Mab.

'It was lucky I had my stick to hand. That's one good thing about being deficient in the leg area, it grows you mighty strong arms, even for someone as old as me.'

So that explained that.

'How long was I under?' Ned put out his hands to the warmth of the fire.

'A few seconds. And then a few seconds more.

It doesn't take long to drown. Or to turn into an ice-block.'

Ned shivered again.

'Cheer up. Here we both are, about to have the famous English cup of tea. Then it's home and that hot bath.'

Ned took the mug of tea Doug was holding out. He watched as the old man added three spoonfuls of sugar from a paper twist.

'I was thinking of Mab.'

'Mab?' It took the old man a moment to remember. 'Ellen's sister, you mean. You don't want to think of that sort of thing now. There's no bringing the dead back. Best concentrate on the living.'

Ned looked at Doug's old face, the pouchy eyes, the weather-beaten skin, the bent and bony old back. The fresh-faced, cheerful Mab who'd become his friend seemed much more part of the 'living' than Doug did. But he decided to keep this thought to himself. He'd never told Doug about Mab's return and this wasn't the time to start now. Grown-ups, even the sharpest, had a curious habit of not believing what was in front of their eyes. Or perhaps they just didn't see.

'Home!' announced Doug. He pulled apart the fire and began to stuff his few belongings into two bags.

'Are you coming with me?'

'What do you think?' Doug raised his arms to indicate the broad and empty sweep of beach, sky and sea.

'You can't stay here.'

They began to walk. Ned's clothes dripped and his

shoes made sucking noises, although since the tea he felt warmer inside. What a fuss his mother would have made! Men were better about things like wet clothes. Things that didn't matter.

His wits were returning and he remembered why he'd searched out Doug. He'd hoped that he would go to the hospital and check out Tony. Danny would trust Doug, for some strange reason. He supposed he should ask him now but it felt enough effort just to walk. With any luck, Danny was still tucked up in bed and hadn't done anything crazy yet – like going into town and being picked up by the police.

'Come on, young man, the sky's not fallen in.'

Ned supposed Doug had misread his anxious expression as reflecting cold and weariness. 'Not yet,' he muttered, knowing the old man would be too deaf to hear.

They continued plodding along together. The way back seemed much further than on Ned's way there. At last the row of pretty houses and cottages came into view.

Ned and Doug stood outside Lilac Cottage. 'Are you coming in?' asked Ned, a little doubtfully.

'I wouldn't say no to a hearty breakfast.'

'Aunt Ellen would definitely want me to invite you in.'

Doug entered almost on tiptoes, a weird sight for a man so tall and thin, and Ned guessed he could hardly believe he was inside his beloved Ellen's house. It was a bit embarrassing, really.

'I'm going upstairs,' he shouted and made an extra noise on the stairs to break the spell. 'The kitchen's through there,' he called over his shoulder, before plunging into the bathroom and turning on the taps.

Only then, he thought of Danny. Where was she? She couldn't have slept through all this racket.

'Danny!' Ned threw open her bedroom door. But only Sid looked up with a startled expression on her face. She opened her mouth wide for a big lazy yawn. 'Where is she, Sid?' If Danny had been downstairs, she'd certainly have come out, particularly when she heard Doug's voice.

Ned bent down to stroke Sid's soft fur. 'She's gone, hasn't she? Well, I've got to get warm. It won't help anyone if I catch pneumonia.'

'Miaow,' responded Sid as if in agreement – although as she jumped off the bed, Ned knew she was probably only asking for her breakfast.

23

There's something particularly cheering about becoming very warm after being very cold. Ned tucked into the huge fry-up produced by Doug, and couldn't help feeling everything would turn out all right.

'You'll need to do some shopping, young man,' warned Doug, looking equally cheerful.

Ned decided not to inform him this was the last of the food bought by Aunt Ellen's fair hands. 'It's still blowing out there,' he said, putting off mention of Danny's departure.

'It's an ill wind that blows nobody any good. You know what, that beach hut being bust into smithereens was the best thing that could have happened to me.'

'You wouldn't have thought so if you'd gone into the sea with it.' Ned couldn't control a shiver as he thought of his recent experience.

'True enough.' Doug wiped the last signs of egg and tomato from his plate with a large piece of bread. 'But as I sat on that cold beach thanking God for a lucky escape, it all became clear to me.'

'Oh, yes.' Sometimes lately, Ned found himself feeling older and more cynical than Doug, even if Doug did have seventy years advance on him.

'I understood I'd been saved so Ellen and I can spend our last years together. Tell me, is there a razor in the house?' He felt his white stubbled chin. 'Got to keep up the good work started by the barber.' From this, Ned gathered the old man had finally decided to claim Ellen as his own. Doubtless he was already planning a white wedding and the moment he'd carry her over the threshold – quite a good idea actually as, from what Ned had seen, she could hardly walk.

Now was the time to tell him about Danny, about the terrifying Phil and the baby sister in hospital. 'I've got something I need help with,' he began, 'but first I'd better fill you in with the background.'

Doug was a good listener. He sat quite still, watching Ned's face. When he'd finished, Doug poured himself another cup of tea and said, 'So you're thinking we might kill two birds with one stone.'

'Hopefully, not kill.'

'Quite. So after I've persuaded Ellen we belong together,' his voice quavered a little here, 'I go visit this baby.'

'Tony,' added Ned helpfully. 'Antoinette, in full.'

There was a pause. Doug drank his tea in a rather noisy, slurpy way. It was his teeth, thought Ned, or actually his false teeth. Ned hoped, for Doug's sake, Ellen was prepared to overlook that sort of thing.

'So where is Danny?' asked Doug.

Somehow Ned had not got round to this bit of information after all.

'Gone.'

'Gone? Gone where? Gone why?'

'Don't know.' Ned looked down at his plate.

'She might have been picked up by now. Could be the best thing, too.'

'You promised you'd never give us away.'

'I won't do that. You choose your own paths. People are always telling children what to do but most often the children know best. You two have looked after each other as good as any adult.'

'But now she's gone.'

'To the hospital?'

'Probably.' Ned began to feel his warm glow departing. 'She didn't have money for a bus. She got here in the back of a lorry. I suppose she could do that again.'

'Brave girl.' Doug clicked his teeth and harrumphed as if he was thinking. 'It seems her worst luck would be if she ran into this Phil.'

'She doesn't want to be put into care,' said Ned.

The old man heaved himself to his feet. 'So what about a razor?'

'I don't think Aunt Ellen was into shaving her legs.' Ned thought it was quite fun teasing Doug. 'And I've not much call for one either.'

'It'll have to be the barber again, then.' Doug buttoned up his tweed jacket and started walking slowly out of the room. He looked very worn and old, and Ned wondered worriedly whether his false bit of leg and foot hurt all the time. 'Are you sure you don't need a rest?'

'I'll be resting underground long enough in a few years. You stay here, in case Danny comes back.' He pulled some money out of his pocket and handed several rather damp notes to Ned. 'And if she does turn up, buy us some food. Potatoes, carrots. Something nourishing from the earth.'

'OK.' Ned decided it would sound cowardly to admit how nervous he was about showing his face in the village.

The cottage seemed very empty once Ned had shut the door behind the old man. It reminded Ned of his first day when he'd had only Sid to keep him company. Then Mab had come. But not till night-time.

The weather outside hadn't improved. He could hear the wind rattling the window frames and pushing at the door. The queer yellowish light still brightened the grey, although in a cheerless, even threatening way.

Probably it would rain soon. He mooched through the kitchen to the larder and began to check out the food situation: one tin soup – asparagus (ugh), one jar beetroot slices (ugh), one tin mandarin oranges (possible), a bag of potatoes (untouched by him and maybe answering the need for Doug's nourishing 'earth' vegetables). There wasn't much else eatable at all and the fridge was equally empty.

Sid had followed him and was twirling her tail

round his legs with her usual greedy intent. 'Don't worry, Sid, there's plenty of cans of cat food for you.' Ned bent down to stroke her.

A sudden shatteringly loud banging on the front door made them both freeze. Sid's fur stood on end and Ned felt his eyes widen with shock and fright.

The cat recovered first and, quick as a flash, leaped on to the shelf and out of the window.

He felt like following her. Why did he have to be brave all the time? Could it be the postman gone haywire? But there had been something deliberate and menacing about the blows on the door.

He unfroze, moved slowly forward, and as he did so, the banging started again as if someone wanted to break down the door. He could hear shouting too, although not the words – a man's deep voice.

Moving even more tentatively, he went through the kitchen, out into the hall briefly and into the living-room. The lace curtains at the windows would protect him from view and maybe he'd get a glimpse of whatever maniac stood outside, or at least hear what he had to say.

Standing anxiously in the little room, he remembered the story of the wolf and the three pigs, and just hoped that the man wouldn't huff and puff and blow his house down. At least Lilac Cottage was built of stone, not straw.

'Open up!' bellowed the man. 'I know you're in there! When I get hold of you, I'll give you a battering like you've never had.'

Trying to stay calm, Ned decided that the man must be very stupid if he thought the promise of a thrashing was more likely to make him open the door. Very, very quietly he tiptoed to the window – not that the man was likely to hear him with the noise he was making.

On the other hand, he wasn't at all sure he had the nerve to lift even the corner of the curtain. His best bet seemed to be to lie low, pray the door held firm and the intruder went away eventually. He retreated back to the middle room, where he concentrated on trying to make his legs stop shaking.

'You think you're so clever, running off like that! I'll never be found, you think! You don't give a toss, do you, what you left behind!' The voice and hammering raised to a new level.

Ned sat on one of the chairs and put two cushions over his legs. He was beginning to suspect who his visitor was, and it didn't make him any happier.

'The police didn't find you, true enough. But they're stupid, aren't they? Don't have the time neither. Not like me, thrown out of the house. All because of you! You stitch, yellow, scum-girl! Wait till I get my hands on you!'

Now he was kicking with his feet as well as pounding with his fists. Ned just hoped it wouldn't occur to him how much less painful it would be to break a window and get in that way.

Luckily, he seemed too angry to think, and was probably drunk too, by the slurring in his words.

This guess was confirmed as Ned heard the sound of a breaking bottle, accompanied by further shouts of fury.

'Ruined my life you have! Lyn won't have me in the house now! Says I drove you out! But I knew I'd find you! Give you a bit of what you deserve!'

Obviously this was Phil. Ned remembered what Danny had said about him, and dragged another cushion over and put it on top of himself, as if that could safeguard him from Phil's wrath. He tried to tell himself it was a good thing Danny wasn't here, but it didn't make him any braver. For the first time, he wished he had some closer neighbours.

'I could find you all right!' bellowed Phil. 'Twelve villages I've been to. Asked about. Everyone knows everything in villages. Children on their own in Lilac Cottage, they told me. I knew straightaway. Bought antiseptic, didn't he, your friend? You learn everything, if you ask the right way! She called you *children*, the puffed-up woman in the chemist who fancies herself, but I call you DEVILS!' He paused, to do some more serious kicking.

Ned tried to calm himself enough to consider his options. They didn't seem good. The most obvious was to ring the police. People can't go kicking other people's doors and get away with it. At least he assumed they couldn't. But if the police came, they'd discover he was living on his own and he'd be whisked off to somewhere he didn't want to go.

He'd held out for such a long time. It would be silly

to give up too easily. So if he didn't call the police, what else could he do?

Phil was rattling at the door handle now. Ned could hear his heavy breathing, even through two walls. It was just possible, he supposed, that once he burst in and found no Danny he'd bunk off again without attacking him. But somehow he doubted it. Phil seemed to be in the kind of mood when he'd take out his fury on anyone who got in his way.

He wasn't hearing any noises from Phil now. The wind was loud enough but not rattling or banging. For a moment his heart lifted: he had given up and gone!

Then he heard the worst sound in the world: a stamping in the hallway. Phil was inside the house!

Ned looked wildly round the room. There was no escape. His only hope was if Phil went up the stairs, giving him a chance to dash out through the front door. But he could hear his breathing again, just the other side of the door. It was more frightening that Phil was invisible and that he, Ned, had never seen him so he couldn't even give him a body or face. Maybe he was like the giant in *Jack and the Beanstalk*. '*Fee fi fo fum, I smell the blood of an Englishman. Be he alive or be he dead, I'll grind his bones to make my bread.*'

Did he have to remember nasty fairy stories at just this moment? What he wanted was to be a brave man of action. And why was Phil taking so long to make up his mind?

Then the bullying voice came again, 'Old trick that, leaving the door unlocked. Made me think you want me inside, set a trap – but I'm not taken in by that. I'm counting to ten, Danny, and then you come out and take what's coming to you! One . . .'

Ned was bewildered. The door unlocked? Then he had a clear image of staggering back with Doug from the beach that morning – and he hadn't had a key, but the door had opened because Danny had unlocked it and gone out without locking it again. Phil could have walked in any time he wanted. If Ned wasn't so frightened, he'd have laughed.

Still, it obviously had made Phil a bit nervous or he would be blasting in, not standing in the hallway counting.

'. . . four . . . five . . .'

If only he knew how to throw his voice, thought Ned – who'd once seen a programme on the subject – he could have pretended to be Danny and called from upstairs. No-go to that.

Then he noticed Doug's stick, left behind to dry. It was leaning against the wall. Very cautiously, Ned got off his chair and crept towards it.

24

'. . . eight . . . nine . . . ten! Here I come, you VERMIN!'

The door was flung open and the monstrously large figure of Phil burst into the room. Danny hadn't described his great size and girth – his belly hung over his trousers like a second person. Ned, crouching in the cupboard at the end of the room (lucky the Prince's Quest board was still on the floor or he'd never have fitted in), stared with horror through a crack at the hinges. Phil's red bulbous face and flat-backed shaven head was like something out of a horror movie.

The next bit happened so quickly that Ned could hardly follow it. In fact the first part went exactly as he'd planned, when he wedged Doug's walking-stick between the two armchairs so that it formed a sturdy trip-wire just inside the room.

As Phil lunged forward, eyes searching for Danny, his foot caught on the stick and he fell heavily to the ground. But it wasn't enough; he was up again, even more ferocious, yelling filthy words.

Ned had nothing to do with what happened next.

Phil's huge foot stepped firmly forward, as if he knew where a child would be hiding. But instead of treading on carpet, he placed it right in the middle of the shiny Prince's Quest board which, acting like the sharpest skate-board, shot forward uncontrollably.

Phil's huge arms waved like a windmill as he tried to recover his balance. His legs stretched wide apart as the front foot shot forward on the board and, in a split-second, he'd slammed into the cupboard so hard that Ned was afraid he'd be smashed into smithereens. Instead, Phil fell backwards. His legs shot up in the air and he came down heavily, his horrible head, mouth open, striking the walking-stick with immense force. There was a splintering sound as it broke, before his head thudded on to the floor.

Then there was silence.

Ned let out a choking gasp. He realised he'd been holding his breath till then. It sounded very loud in the quiet room. Phil was still lying where he'd fallen. He must be unconscious. Or was he pretending?

Cautiously, Ned pushed the cupboard door open a centimetre. No movement from the floor. Very slowly he put out one cramped leg, then a hand, keeping his eyes on Phil all the time. How long did someone stay unconscious – if that's what he was. Maybe he was *dead*. The idea struck Ned with a different kind of horror. He wouldn't like to have killed a man – even Phil.

Now he had to get out and look. It only took a quick glance to see the vast stomach was moving up and down as Phil breathed. So what would happen when he came to? And was it his duty to ring for an ambulance? But then the police would certainly come too.

Phil presented nearly as many problems unconscious as conscious. But at least he wasn't frightening any more – just disgusting. Ned looked down at his huge body – a hairy chest was visible where his T-shirt had ridden up – and wondered whatever Danny's mum could have seen in him.

As if on cue, steps approached from the front door – a child's light steps – and a very scared face peered into the room.

'Ned,' whispered Danny, 'did Phil come here?' She hadn't yet seen who lay on the floor.

'Sure he did,' whispered Ned, with what he guessed was a triumphant grin. 'Sure he came and, what's more, he's still here!' He pointed to the floor.

Danny did a double-take and jumped about a metre in the air. 'Yerks!'

'He won't hurt you,' said Ned.

She crept back again. 'Is he dead?'

'No such luck,' said Ned laconically. 'He's just unconscious. He fell backwards, hit his head.'

Danny put out a finger tentatively, as if she might test-prod him, and then retracted it quickly. Ned saw she was fingering her still-bruised face, as if remembering how it had felt when Phil had landed those blows.

'What happens when he wakes up?' she said.

'That's the thousand-dollar question.' They were both whispering and Ned lowered his voice still further. 'He won't feel too hot with that bang on his head plus all the drink inside him.'

Danny nodded. 'I saw that broken bottle. He's always worse when he's drunk. I saw him at the shops, see. I didn't know what to do. But I guessed he might come here.' She looked up at Ned and then gestured to the comatose body of Phil. 'How did he get like this?'

'It began with me tripping him and ended with him knocking himself out.'

'Not bad for a little guy!' exclaimed Danny admiringly. 'You never told me how enormous he was.'

'Didn't I?' Ned could see Danny was recovering her nerve. She gave a shove at Phil's leg with her trainer.

'Never kick a man who's down.' Ned began to laugh.

'Sshh,' said Danny severely. 'I'll tell you what I think. I think we've got to tie him up.'

'Tie him up! What with? He's so strong, he'd break anything.'

'What if he wakes up and goes mad?'

'Mightn't he have had enough?' said Ned hopefully. 'Mightn't he just go? We could hide outside so he couldn't get us.'

'You want him to smash up your Aunt Ellen's nice house, do you? That's what he'll do, for sure. You still don't get it, do you, Ned? He's like a wild animal when he's angry!'

'Well, what could we tie him with?'

Danny thought. 'There's the skipping-rope.'

'Suppose that could do his wrists,' said Ned doubtfully, 'but I've never been any good at knots. And if he gets free, he'll be even angrier. Anyway, we can't keep him here for ever.'

'We'll tie him up and drag him outside,' hissed Danny determinedly, 'and then we'll put him on the beach and hope a giant wave carries him out to sea so he can be eaten by sharks.'

'We'll never get him that far,' objected Ned, trying not to smile at Danny's malicious expression. 'He must weigh a ton.'

But Danny had already gone out of the room. She returned a moment or two later with the skipping-rope.

Using their combined strength, they managed to shift Phil enough to get his arms behind his back and wind the rope round his wrists. Neither of them had a clue about the proper knots for prisoners, so they tied a whole bunch of granny knots one on top of the other.

'That has to hold,' said Danny. 'Now for his legs. He's got a kick like a buffalo.'

'You watch. I'll look for another rope.' Leaving Danny to guard Phil, Ned hurried through to the kitchen. Taking no notice of the mess he was making, he'd pulled out every drawer and rummaged through every cupboard. He was just heading for the larder when Danny appeared.

'He's stirring,' she hissed. 'Get a move on!'

'Can't find anything,' hissed back Ned, despairingly.

'We could stab him.' Danny went over to one of the open drawers where there were several large sharp knives.

'Don't be stupid!' Ned feared she might be serious.

They both turned with the same expression of terror, as there was a definite sound of movement from the living-room.

'Hello, you two. Who is that monster on the floor?' It was Mab, bright and well-turned-out as ever.

Ned and Danny didn't know whether to laugh or scream.

'It's Phil!' exclaimed Danny.

'We need a rope!' begged Ned. 'You'll know where Aunt Ellen keeps her ropes.'

Mab went straight to the larder. She returned with a large, neatly wound length of cord. 'Washing-line,' she announced matter-of-factly.

'You're a star!' breathed Danny.

'I expect you want me to tie him up too. As it happens, I was a keen member of the Brownies before the war. Let's see. What we need is the sort of slipknot that tightens if a person pulls on it.'

Mab returned to the living-room, where she bent over Phil. He was grunting a little, and now and again his eyes flickered.

Mab undid the washing-line carefully and threaded it between his feet.

'Quick!' urged Danny nervously.

'More haste, less speed.' Mab threaded the long cord up round Phil's shoulders and down again. She didn't get flustered even when he gave a sudden heave and one eye opened, showing a glaring red eyeball. Luckily, he subsided again.

'Now get me the longer half of that stick.'

Asking no questions – Mab seemed to know exactly what she was doing – Danny disengaged the larger remains of Doug's stick from under an armchair and brought it to Mab.

Deftly, as if she'd done it a thousand times before, Mab slotted it down Phil's back, behind the ropes. 'Now he won't even be able to sit up,' she announced with satisfaction.

'Like a trussed chicken!' celebrated Danny.

'More like a wild boar,' said Ned. He stared down. Although he was extremely glad to see Phil put out of action, he did wonder whether tying someone up like this amounted to torture. 'Is he in pain?' he whispered to Mab.

'Only from the drink and the bang on his head,' answered Mab cheerfully. 'Both self-inflicted.'

'I wish he was in huge pain,' gloated Danny. 'Couldn't we barbecue him on nice hot coals?'

At that moment both of Phil's eyes opened together, and a second later he let out a great roar. All three children jumped backwards. Even Mab lost her cool. 'We should have gagged him,' she said.

A stream of filthy words poured from Phil's mouth, and the children watched as he began to pull and struggle against his bonds. He was so agitated that he didn't seem to notice them nor have any idea where he was. His eyes swivelled wildly, and every now and again he let out another roar.

'He really is like an animal,' whispered Ned.

'Think of having him as a stepfather,' returned Danny.

Suddenly Phil's eyes stopped their crazed revolving and began to focus. 'Danny?' It was a deep growl.

Danny stepped forward, confident now the ropes would hold. 'Yes, it's me. It's Danny. And you can't do a thing about it. I could do all sorts of horrible things to you but I'm not going to.'

Well, that's a relief, thought Ned.

'Because I'm not like you and I don't take pleasure in hurting people weaker than me,' continued Danny.

'Where am I?' mumbled Phil.

'You're in my friend's house. Or at least his great-aunt's. Where you came with *evil intent*.' Danny brought out the words with a good deal of relish. 'But now you've met your match.'

'I feel terrible,' moaned Phil. 'I might be dying.'

'No, you're not. In a minute, we're going to drag you outside and dump you like an old bit of garbage.'

'What? What do you mean? Who tied me up?'

'Someone who knows their knots.' Danny looked around as if to point out Mab but, as Ned had noticed a minute or two earlier, she'd gone. Having served her purpose, she'd left them to deal with the rest.

'This is Ned,' finished Danny, with a bit of an anticlimax.

'Kids!' grimaced Phil.

'We may be kids,' said Danny, smiling nastily, 'but you still can't move hand or foot.' To which truth Phil responded with a frustrated bellow.

Ned tugged at Danny's elbow.

'What is it?' Danny didn't turn or take her eyes off Phil. Clearly, she didn't want to miss a moment of Phil's humiliation.

Ned dragged her over to the window and whispered in her ear. 'How are we going to get rid of him?' It was becoming dark already and the waves were making a great noise.

'Do what we said.' Danny seemed impatient. 'Haul him outside.'

'We'd need a tractor to do that.' He looked away. 'Perhaps we should ring the police . . .'

'If you do that, I'll kill you! Then I'll kill myself!' Danny grabbed Ned's arm and pinched it so hard he nearly screamed.

'I don't want them either,' he stuttered out. 'You know that.'

'Then don't talk about it. The police are out!' Danny had raised her voice, and Ned and she became aware of a new turmoil from the floor. They both turned to look.

'Who's talking about the police?' yelled Phil hoarsely. 'I'm not staying for no police. Get me out of here.' He began to struggle energetically, and suddenly Ned had a brainwave. First he signalled to Danny to keep quiet, then he stepped up to Phil.

'You overheard right,' he said boldly. 'The police'll be here any minute. I rang them when you knocked yourself out. They're very keen to talk to you.'

'You can't do this.' His voice had changed to a whine. 'I didn't hurt you, did I?'

185

Ned didn't even bother to answer that one. 'They're just longing to get you, that's all I know.' He could see his words were hitting home because Phil had stopped struggling and was looking almost pale, although his large nose stayed revoltingly mottled.

'I didn't take nothing much, did I?' He was begging now. 'It's her mum's fault, isn't it? Throwing me out. I have to eat, don't I? Those supermarkets make millions. Why would they care about a bit of this and that? And last night, I had to sleep somewhere, didn't I? How was I to know there were people in the house? They should've left a light on.'

Ned didn't quite take in these remarks until Danny yelled, 'Thief! Burglar!'

'You wait till I get free!' A bit of the old Phil reasserted itself. Danny jumped backwards. Ned gave her a warning look. If his plan were to work, she mustn't provoke him too far. It was obvious he found it hard enough to think sensibly, and quite impossible when he was in a red rage.

'OK, Phil.' Ned tried to sound manful, firm but fair. 'You know you're wanted by the police. We know you're wanted by the police. You're in a bad way. At our mercy. But there is one way out of the mess for you.'

'What's that?' moaned Phil.

'If we let you go before the police arrive.'

'What!' shrieked Danny.

'Ssshh!' hissed Ned.

'You'll do that?' Phil looked unconvinced, as well he might with Danny grimacing furiously at him.

186

'Of course, you won't hang around to meet the police.' Ned tried to give Danny a meaningful look. After all, there were no police. If Phil believed it, it would a giant con and he'd be out of their hair.

'We just want to get rid of you,' said Ned, 'but you'd better make up your mind quickly or they'll be here.'

At last Danny seemed to get the point. She went to the door, then called back, 'Is that a siren I hear? Yeah. It just might be. Coming nearer.'

'Ergh. Quick! Let me out!' Phil's terror was a pleasure to behold.

Ned bent to start the untying process. Phil stank revoltingly of whisky and sweat.

'Can't you get a move on?' He was definitely panicking.

The trouble was, Mab had tied the knots and Ned had no idea how to untie them.

'Getting closer!' called Danny gleefully from the door.

'Find a knife, can't you?' Phil was writhing on the floor which made Ned's job no easier. A knife seemed the only answer.

Apologising inwardly to Aunt Ellen for destroying her skipping-rope and her washing-line, Ned went to the kitchen and returned with a carving knife.

A few slashes and Phil was free. Ned couldn't believe how quickly he was on his feet and heading for the door. He only paused for a second to aim a swipe at Danny, which she easily ducked, before lumbering off along the front.

Ned joined Danny and they both watched till he was

187

as small as a toy man weaving his way against the wind.

'We saw him off all right!' announced Danny with satisfaction. She kicked the pieces of broken bottle to the side and then gave Ned a high five.

'We sure did,' he agreed, smiling.

'First time the police came in useful,' she added as they came into Lilac Cottage and shut and locked the door.

'In their absence,' commented Ned.

It was only when they'd gone through to the kitchen that Ned thought to himself that although they'd seen off Phil in style, he now knew where Danny was staying and might come back at any time.

Naturally, he didn't share this nasty idea with Danny.

'So where's the food?' asked Danny, opening the fridge door.

'There isn't any,' replied Ned. Even good moments aren't perfect.

25

A bang on the front door was the very last thing Ned and Danny wanted to hear. It came about an hour after Phil's abrupt departure.

Ned and Danny had just finished clearing up the mess in the living-room and were eating some strange-tasting biscuits they'd found in a cupboard. Danny was in the middle of asking, 'Are you sure these aren't cat biscuits?' and Ned was planning to answer, 'They taste so fishy you're probably right,' when the banging came.

'It doesn't sound at all like Phil,' announced Ned bravely.

'Fine. You can answer it, then.'

'OK.' Ned went to the door and said, 'H-hello.' The stutter let him down a bit but he was still pleased by how calm he sounded.

'You two taken to booze?' replied a friendly voice.

'It's Doug!' Ned called back to Danny.

'Who's Doug?'

'I told you. He's the old man.' Ned unlocked and opened the door.

Danny hadn't seen Doug since his transformation from disreputable tramp to respectable citizen. She stared at him in amazement.

'Hey, look at you, all posh in your new coat!'

'Thank you, young lady. You wouldn't have a cup of tea for a parched old man?'

'We would,' answered Ned, 'as long as you don't ask for milk or anything to eat.'

'But I gave you money for food.' Looking disappointed, Doug lowered himself into an armchair.

So Ned and Danny told him the dramatic story of their visitor and owned up to the broken walking-stick. 'That's why we got scared when you knocked.'

'You're afraid he might revisit the scene of the crime?' asked Doug. 'Don't worry about the stick. I'm not planning on using it much in the future.' He paused. 'While we're on the subject, you should clear away that broken bottle. It looks and smells terrible.' He paused again and seemed almost to be smiling. 'What would your Aunt Ellen think if she should happen to come back?'

'You don't mean . . . !' exclaimed Ned.

'I saw her.' The old man sat back in his chair, closed his eyes and a look of ecstasy came over his ancient wrinkled face.

Ned saw Danny giving him a funny look, or maybe she was worrying about the Phil situation.

'Did she recognise you? After all, it is sixty years.'

'Sixty years!' exclaimed Danny.

'Yes, she did,' answered Doug simply. 'She was asleep

when I arrived so I sat on the chair and waited. Ten minutes passed. I was so happy to be with her, I wouldn't have minded what happened next.'

'But didn't she look horribly *old* to you?' persisted Ned, who remembered Doug's description of the girl with rose-petal skin etc., etc.

'No. She looked neither old nor young. She was just herself, Ellen, *my* Ellen.'

'Ugh,' commented Danny.

Doug smiled at her. 'My apologies, dear friend.'

'Don't be put off by her,' said Ned. 'She's *my* aunt and *I* want to know what happened.'

'No offence meant but I'm leaving.' Danny got off her chair and left the room. Ned heard her stamping up the stairs.

'I don't blame her,' said Doug, still smiling. 'It's an absurd story.'

'Danny's upset,' said Ned. 'But I want to hear. Go on.'

Doug took on his ecstatic expression again. 'Ellen opened her eyes and looked at me perfectly calmly with no sense of surprise. She said, "I was dreaming, then I wake up and here you are. Am I still dreaming? Are you like Mab, who comes to me when I need her?"

'So I took hold of her frail little hand and leaned forward, "I'm not dead, Ellen. I never was. My plane crashed and I lost my memory." I didn't tell her about my foot or too many details because I could see she was finding it hard enough to take in it was truly *me* sitting there.

'Then she said, "So you've come back to me."'

'And I said, "I'm never going to leave you again."'

'So that's the way it is, more or less. I talked to her doctor later, who promised me there was no serious reason to keep her in hospital. She just needs someone to look after her, plus regular physio. I told him I could look after her and when he gave me a bit of an up-and-downer, I said I'd get extra nursing help too.'

'That's great.' Ned tried to smile back at this weird old romantic who'd come so suddenly into his life. But he couldn't help wondering how they'd all fit into Lilac Cottage. Doug was very tall, if skinny, and there was Danny too. Ned was reminded of the mission he'd given Doug. He'd just ask him straight out.

'Did you look for Danny's baby sister?'

'Oh, my!'

From the expression on Doug's face, Ned knew that he'd forgotten.

'What a selfish old man I am! That's what comes of living alone for so long, you don't think of anyone but yourself.'

He looked so downcast that Ned felt sorry for him. 'I didn't tell Danny you were going,' he said. 'She's not expecting any news. In fact she'd set off for the hospital herself but Phil turned up on the scene.'

'Of course, I'll be going in tomorrow.' Doug drummed his bony fingers on the side of the armchair as if he wished he could set off that moment. 'I inquired in the village on my way and I've found a good fellow who'll act as my driver.'

Ned stared at Doug in astonishment. Didn't he realise that asking round the village would almost certainly give him and Danny away to everybody. Doug had promised not to tell anyone, right from the beginning. This was as good as telling. Obviously, his new respectability and finding Aunt Ellen had wiped everything else out of his head.

'But what about us?' Ned exclaimed, trying not to sound too childishly whining.

'You? You're hungry, aren't you?' The old man hadn't got the point at all.

Ned thought more. The truth was that, as far as he was concerned, everything had changed. He had been lying low in Lilac Cottage because he didn't want to: a) bother his parents, b) be sent away to a bullying cousin. Or maybe in reverse order. But now Aunt Ellen was coming back and, even before she arrived, Doug would be staying in the cottage. So no one would try and send him away anyway.

On the other hand, it was quite another matter for Danny. A whole lot of people would be the last thing she wanted. She was still in hiding.

'I didn't mean food,' said Ned, 'although now you mention it, I'm ravenous. I was worrying about Danny.'

'Don't you fret, we'll look after Danny.' Doug's voice was perfectly carefree.

'The point is,' Ned tried again, 'Danny's terrified—'

He didn't get any further before Doug had stood up and placed a calming hand on Ned's arm – although Ned couldn't help noticing it was more like a claw than

193

a hand. 'Give things time, young man. Tomorrow I'll bring news of her sister.'

If you remember, thought Ned.

'Just now I'm off in search of food. There must be a famous British fish and chip shop in a village by the sea.'

After he'd gone, Ned went slowly upstairs. He knocked on Danny's bedroom door – soon to be Great-Aunt Ellen's again.

'Come in.' It wasn't Danny's voice.

Mab was seated on the end of the bed, Danny huddled so far under the bedclothes that Ned could only see a few strands of hair. 'You came back!'

'She needs me.'

'I tried to help.' Ned looked down at his feet. 'I got rid of Phil.'

'He's still out there somewhere.'

'Doug's here now. He's gone out for fish and chips.'

'Let's hope he's not blown away.'

Mab really was in a funny mood. Ned had forgotten the wild wind that had so nearly blown him out to sea. Phil had been the nearest thing to an inland tempest and Ned hadn't been outside since.

'Doug's old but he's strong. At least his arms are strong. He pulled me out from under a real roller this morning.'

'Quite so,' replied Mab, as if she knew all about it.

'Won't he be surprised to see you!' Ned added. It struck him that 'surprise' was an understatement when a man in his eighties met a girl he'd last seen sixty years ago and found she hadn't aged one bit.

'Oh, he won't see me,' said Mab airily.

'Are you going so soon?'

'It's not that. Doug doesn't need me. When people don't need me, they can't see me. Particularly grown-ups.'

So, *he* still needed her. Well, he did. Everything was extremely confusing, and he wished Danny would come up from under the bedclothes.

'I'm going to check out the weather.' Ned crossed to his own bedroom and the moment he opened the door, was struck by a gale-force wind. The window had come open again and huge gusts were blowing in. He crouched on the bed and tried to close the window. It was like fighting with some great noisy animal, more frightening because it had no shape and came from no one place, roaring in from first one direction and then another. He didn't want to imagine what the sea must be like. No wonder Mab worried about Doug.

The wind dropped for a split-second and he managed to bang shut the window. There was an urgent knock on the front door. What if it was Phil? But it wasn't a crazy banging. He bounded down the stairs. 'Coming!'

The door crashed wide the moment he unlatched it and Doug staggered in out of the darkness.

'They all thought I was crazy coming out in this weather and I agreed.'

He looked very odd. His white hair stood on end

and his face was nearly as pale as his hair, except for his long purple nose. He'd also become strangely fat with his smart tweed jacket straining each button across his chest.

'Are you all right?' asked Ned, in the way people do when someone is obviously not all right – or not *very* all right, anyway.

'It's mayhem out there. The waves are like skyscrapers. I hardly expected Lilac Cottage to be standing. Come on now! Forward to the kitchen.'

In the kitchen, Doug unbuttoned his jacket to reveal a plastic bag stuffed with fish and chips. 'Better than a hot-water bottle,' he pronounced with satisfaction. From his pockets he produced a packet of gherkins, a bottle of vinegar, several packets of salt, and a carton of milk. Ned found his mouth was watering. At the smell, Sid – who Ned hadn't seen since Phil's entry – hurtled into the kitchen mewing plaintively.

'Plenty for all!' Doug dropped a large piece of fish on the floor, which Sid pounced on greedily.

'Go to it, then.'

As they all tucked in, Doug paused. 'Where's our female friend?'

'I'll call her.' Actually Ned doubted if Danny would come down, but he went to the bottom of the staircase and called, then, when there was no answer, went upstairs and into her room. It was pretty kind, considering how much he was enjoying the fish and chips.

Danny was still buried under the blankets. There

was no sign of Mab. 'Food's on the table.' Ned's voice seemed too loud. He bent close to Danny and from what little he could see, decided she was deeply asleep. That must be the reason Mab felt she could safely leave her.

Back in the kitchen, Doug was in high spirits. Ned supposed that his victory over the weather had made him feel young again – plus the continuing Aunt Ellen factor, of course.

Between them they'd soon polished off the fish and chips.

'I shall push together those two armchairs in the living-room.' Doug stood up. 'Leaving a gap which I will stack with cushions. Care to help?'

'Certainly, sir.' Ned could have offered Doug his bed, but it was a very small bed, and he seemed so enthusiastic about his own plan.

When they'd finished creating this rather strange bed, Doug announced that he'd be washing in the kitchen sink. So Ned kept out of his way for a bit. He wondered if one of Doug's plastic bags held a pair of pyjamas, and then felt curious about his false foot. Would he remove it before sleep? And his false teeth?

All in all, it was embarrassing to be at such close quarters with the old man, and he was relieved when Doug went into the living-room and announced, 'I'm turning in. Even my old ears can hear there's a storm like a train approaching outside the window, but nothing could stop me sleeping tonight. Tomorrow is another day, and the sooner I get to your dear Aunt Ellen the better.' He put an arm on Ned's shoulder and pushed him towards the door. 'I advise you, young man, to follow my example.'

With this, he closed the door. Ned stood outside for a moment. If Doug had his way, he would soon have a great-uncle as well as a great-aunt. He wandered into the kitchen and ate a few cold chips lurking in the paper bag. He should go to bed – it was already ten o'clock and the storm was winding its way into the house, so he felt cold as well as tired. But some feeling of being on guard was keeping him awake. Clearly, Doug had no such worries. Regular snores were already coming through the wall between the kitchen and living-room. There hadn't been a sound from Danny above.

Sid, replete with fish, was lying under the table. 'Come here, Sid, and keep me warm.' What was he waiting up for? Ned didn't really know. It seemed most unlikely that anyone, even someone as out of control as Phil, would come out in this weather. Yet he still sat at the table, although after a bit his head nodded as he fell into a light doze.

Sid was the first to alert him. She dashed out from under the table and stood, legs and tail rigid, fur on end, a deep fierce growl coming from her throat. Her tail began to lash his leg.

He jumped up. 'What is it?' He went dazedly to the kitchen door and opened it. At first he could only hear the wind gusting against the front door and, closer at hand, Doug's snores. He listened harder and made out a distinct tapping; a deliberate, although not loud, knocking.

At Ned's side, Sid's growling turned into a hissing.

26

As Ned had learned over the last days on his own, there's no way you can avoid taking action, not for long anyway.

Warily, with Sid winding between his legs – at least she hadn't run away this time – Ned approached the front door. 'Who's there?' He had to speak quite loudly for his voice to rise above the wind. He listened, and there was an answering voice – but too soft for him to hear.

'I'm not letting you in,' he shouted, 'till I know who you are!'

'Ned!' This time the person was yelling. 'Don't you recognise your own dad?'

For a moment Ned couldn't take it in. Dad? Here! He'd felt so on his own and thought about his parents so little that it was almost as if they didn't exist. How could his father be a metre or two away? Surely he was the other side of the world?

'Ned. Hurry and open up, unless you want me to be blown out to sea and drowned!'

Ned opened the door.

'Dad!' It certainly was him, soaking wet and stamping his feet. 'It's raining now,' mumbled Ned.

'Of course it's raining, although I'm not sure it isn't spray from the waves too.' He stood in the hallway, every part of him dripping, including his back-pack which he took off and laid on the floor. He leaned forward and, wet as he was, gave Ned a big hug. 'Hi, Neddy. It's great to see you!'

Ned withdrew a little. 'Hi.'

'So where's your aunt? Asleep is she?' He took in that Ned was fully dressed. 'But you're still up. Don't tell me Ellen's invested in a television?'

'No, Dad . . .' Ned didn't know how he could begin to explain the situation. His immediate problem was stopping his father bursting into the living-room where he'd find an ancient ex-tramp with one leg. One and a half legs. That would take some explaining. Luckily, he could still hear the snores.

'Why don't we go into the kitchen? You can take off your wet things there.'

'Good idea.' Ned's dad, who sometimes liked to be called by his name, Guy, followed Ned obediently. 'You know Neddy, I think you've grown,' he said when they arrived in the kitchen.

'I'll put on the kettle,' said Ned. He knew this line about growing was a real compliment, but he refused to look too pleased. Short or tall, he'd been running his own life for quite a while now.

Guy stripped off his outer clothes and began to rub

his hair with a tea towel Ned handed him. 'Quite a surprise, my arrival, I expect. Your mum and I felt a bit worried about you. Can't think why. Weather aside, nothing could be quieter or safer than Lilac Cottage. So we agreed I'd come ahead. She needs a few more days before she can fly. I hope you haven't been too bored?'

While Ned tried to work out how to answer this one, he got two mugs from the cupboard. On the whole, diversion seemed best. 'Tea or coffee?'

'Coffee. Judging by the way you know this kitchen, you've been helping out your aunt.'

Ned didn't answer this either. Well, it wasn't exactly a question. Luckily, Doug had brought milk at the same time as the fish and chips. 'Milk in your coffee?'

'Sure.' Guy settled down at the table. He looked tired. Hardly surprising after a twenty-four hour flight.

'So how's Mum?' asked Ned, still playing for time. He hesitated before adding, 'And the b-baby?' To his annoyance, he stammered on the 'b'. Well, it was extraordinary to think that last time he'd seen his father they'd been a family of three, and now they were four.

'She's beautiful!' Guy answered with great enthusiasm, but Ned noticed he was a little diverted, as if his mind was on something else.

'Has she a name yet?' asked Ned.

'Rowena or Petronella.'

'You're joking!' The awfulness of the names didn't stop Ned from noticing that his dad had taken up a listening mode.

'Tell me,' said Guy, 'has Aunt Ellen acquired a dog?'

'A dog!' What could he be getting at?

'It's just that I can hear a snorting noise from next door, the sound big dogs make when they're asleep.'

'Big dogs,' repeated Ned stupidly.

'Yes. Alsatians or Great Danes. Perhaps she wanted a guard dog?'

Ned saw that his father wasn't very convinced by his own theory. The image of tiny frail old Aunt Ellen taking an Alsatian for a walk almost made him smile. Sighing, he decided that the time had come to embark on at least one part of his story.

'The thing is, Dad . . . Guy.' He'd try speaking man to man. 'Aunt Ellen hasn't acquired a dog, but she has acquired a fiancé.'

'A fiancé!' Ned had never seen his dad so surprised in his whole life. His blue eyes looked at his son with a mixture of disbelief and pity. Probably he thought he'd gone mad.

'He's called Doug and he's sleeping on two chairs in the living-room. It's him you can hear snoring. He's very old – as old as Aunt Ellen.' Ned paused. He didn't think he should describe more, and it certainly wasn't the moment to give a leg count.

'I'm, I'm gob-smacked!' Guy ran his fingers through his drying hair so it stood up in yellow peaks. 'Why didn't you tell me when I rang?'

Ned decided a certain amount of truth might help. 'It only happened yesterday. I mean they only met yesterday.'

'They only met yesterday and now they're engaged? Ned, get a grip!'

They both jumped as a particularly loud, extended snore came through the wall.

'They knew each other before. You can go and see for yourself,' he added, feeling a little desperate.

'I'm whacked.' Guy gave a yawn. 'I didn't expect all this.'

'Sorry,' said Ned, although he didn't see how he could be blamed. 'You can sleep in my bed, if you want.'

'That's kind.' He paused, frowning. 'Maybe I'll save the fiancé for the morning.'

'Good idea,' agreed Ned, thinking that way he wouldn't have to explain Aunt Ellen's absence and Danny's presence till later.

'These long flights take it out of you.' Rubbing his eyes, Guy got to his feet.

Ned took his bag, which wasn't that heavy, and led him upstairs.

'I still think this fiancé extremely odd,' Guy said as they reached the bedroom door.

'Honestly, he's very nice.' Ned more or less pushed his father into the room. The last thing he wanted was for Danny to wake up.

'But where will *you* sleep?' mumbled Guy, who seemed more or less asleep already.

'Don't worry, I'll find somewhere.' Ned shut the door on him firmly. When the coast was clear, he could sneak in to Danny and share the bed with her – or at least grab a pillow and an eiderdown.

Sitting in the kitchen on his own, Ned began to take in the fact that his dad had arrived and that he wasn't on his own any more. At first it had been yet another shock, causing him more problems, confessions etc. But he could imagine that in the morning his dad, who was a very practical man, would sort things out without too much trouble. Independence was all very well but, come to think of it, he could do with a bit of help.

Judging his father would be well and truly asleep by now, Ned went slowly up the stairs. Above Doug's remorseless snores, he could hear the storm. It was reaching that shrieking sound that had panicked him before.

Very gently, so as not to give Danny a fright, Ned turned the door handle to the bedroom and stepped inside. It was dark, of course, so he waited till his eyes began to see faint outlines and then moved towards the bed.

'Danny. It's me.' He bent closer. He put out a hand. A terrible feeling started in his stomach. No one was in the bed. Danny had gone.

27

This was serious. Danny must have heard his father's arrival and decided to run away. It was crazy, but when had Danny done anything that wasn't crazy? Besides, since the appearance of Phil and then Doug, she'd acted weirdly, refusing to leave her bedroom or even her bed.

With a horrible sense of dread, he remembered the bruised, filthy, frightened creature he'd found in the fisherman's shed. She'd been more like a hunted animal than a human. She'd changed gradually and become cheerier – Ned pictured her practising on the skipping-rope – she'd become a *friend*. But now he'd let her go again, out into the night, out into the storm.

Ned went to get his jacket. He must search for her immediately.

Outside, he was nearly knocked over by gusts of wind and rain. It was cold too, a kind of bitter wetness that would penetrate his clothes whatever he did. He might as well give up trying to stay dry and instead keep warm by moving quickly.

He felt sure that Danny would have gone back to the fishermen's sheds. He was the only one who knew that was where she'd been hiding, so she'd feel fairly safe.

It was hard to make progress against the wind, and the tide was so high that the waves were far closer up the beach than he'd ever known them.

Remembering his morning's experience at the other end of the beach, and the destruction of Aunt Ellen's bathing-hut, he just hoped the tide wouldn't carry the sea as far as the fishermen's sheds. That was just too scary to think about.

For a moment, he wondered if he'd been a fool to set off on his own. But his father had been out on his feet, and Doug might have strong arms but you couldn't say the same for his legs.

Ned found the wind was blowing him first in one direction then the other, so that he was progressing in a zigzag, like a boat tacking. Just as his dad had said, when he got too near the sea, the rain was joined by a good dousing of spray.

Curiously, although the sky was filled with clouds racing about in a most uncontrolled way, the night wasn't entirely black. He supposed that somewhere behind the clouds lurked a moon and stars, bright enough to shine through cracks or more transparent vaporous trails.

He was beginning to get used to the colossal noise, but the whole scene became much more frightening when, in one of these brighter periods, he saw quite clearly the advancing army of waves. What had Doug called them? 'Skyscrapers.' And truly he'd never seen water massed so high. The height had doubled since the morning – and that had been bad enough.

Up till now, Ned hadn't bothered to call for Danny but, suddenly terrified at what might have happened to her, he screamed, 'Danny! Danny! Danny!'

When his throat became hoarse and, of course, there'd been no response, he stopped. At last he could make out a more solid darkness where the sheds stood. To his great relief, the sea was still some metres away, although it seemed to be lapping at the old fishing boat where he'd stood his first morning at Seaburgh.

He pushed himself slowly forward. Sometimes it felt more as if he was going backwards. Little by little, with the wind a siren in his ears, his clothes as wet as a sponge and his feet like two cold stones, he reached the huts. It felt less like a hurricane in their shelter, although they were creaking and swaying as if they wanted to take off into the sky like Dorothy's house in *The Wizard of Oz*.

Feeling along the ridged wooden walls of the first shed, Ned advanced on the third. Danny had to be there!

Just as he reached the door, one of the brighter flashes of light showed him two shocking sights. First, he saw a huge wave burst on to the far side of the boat, its white spray shining brilliantly several metres over the deck. Then, and he only caught a moment of this before everything was dark again, he saw a pair of trainers on the beach.

Perhaps he had been mistaken? Perhaps the giant fountain of spray had confused him. Frantically, he pushed at the door. He didn't want to believe his eyes. The door opened easily and, as he stepped inside, the noise level dropped a little.

'Danny, are you there?'

But he knew she wasn't. It was the emptiest space in the world. In his heart of hearts, he knew those were Danny's trainers and that, just as Aunt Ellen had done sixty years ago, she had decided to end it all and throw herself into the sea.

He ran out of the shed. Tears mingled with the rain on his face. He'd never felt so helpless. What could he do? If he called, she wouldn't hear him. Yet he couldn't leave her, not even to get help.

Slipping and sliding on the pebbles – once even falling right over – he made his way down the beach to where he thought he'd seen the trainers. But it was dark all the way and he couldn't be sure he was going in the right direction. Nor did he know what he expected if he did find them: a note perhaps? Unlikely. Danny wasn't the writing sort.

As he stumbled forward, he was aware of the boat ahead. It became higher as he grew closer, and every now and again another massive wave burst over it, soaking him all over again – except he was so wet already, he couldn't be any wetter.

He'd reach the boat before he found the shoes. He

paused, and at that moment the clouds parted, and by a single shaft of the moon, he saw something move on the stern of the boat.

He couldn't be sure, and it was dark again in a moment, but he thought it was a human figure, a *small* human figure.

He made the last metres in as many seconds. The boat loomed above. He remembered that before he'd clambered on from the sea side, where the boat dipped lower. But he couldn't do that now unless he wanted to be swept away by a wave – which he absolutely definitely did not.

Then he saw a rope dangling down the side. Using his feet against the side of the boat, he began to climb up. Once he nearly got knocked off as a wave broke over his head, but he managed to pull himself over the ledge and fell, spread-eagled, on the bottom of the boat. He still clung on to the rope.

'Ned. Ned.' He wasn't dreaming. It really was her voice.

'Danny?'

'Yes. It's me.' She was beside him, crouching down. so as not to be thrown off the boat.

Ned tried to see her face. 'What happened? I was afraid—'

'Yes. I'd had enough, see.'

'Oh, Danny.' Ned couldn't think of anything to say.

'It's true.'

'You ran away when Dad—'

'Your dad! I thought . . . What with the police, Phil,

even that mad old fellow, I'd had enough. I just went. Like I was.'

Ned realised that a strange noise he'd been hearing was Danny's teeth chattering with cold. 'You can have my coat but it's soaked through.'

'Just stay close. That'll do. I ran straight here, not thinking, just running. The wind was that strong I could hardly breathe. Hurt my teeth. Funny that. I got here though. I was crazy as the storm. I slid down the beach, right as far as the edge. Huge breakers there were, seemed like great battleships; snap you in two, easy. But I wasn't frightened. Not one bit. If she hadn't come, I'd be food for fishes right now.'

'Who? What do you mean?' The wind sometimes took Danny's voice away so that Ned could hardly hear.

'Her. Mab. I heard her voice first. Then I felt her fingers on my arm. She was so strong. I couldn't move forward into the sea however hard I tried.'

'Did she speak?' asked Ned.

'Just "No". Like that. "No." Like no one could go against her. Every time I tried to shake loose, she said that "No" like a bell in my ear. "No!" I suppose in the end I just gave up. She was too much for me. So I let her give me a great push up the beach. It was funny though. I couldn't really see her. I thought I did at first. But it was just her voice and then the grip of her fingers. She wasn't there like you are.'

'She saved you,' said Ned. So Mab – or a sort of Mab – could go outside Lilac Cottage when she was really needed. He raised his head a little to look at the rain-washed boat. 'However did you get up here?'

'I was fighting my way up the beach, like I told you, then a giant wave came and next thing I knew I'd been washed right up here. It felt safer, I can tell you.'

'I was looking for you.' Ned made out Danny's pale face. Her eyes looked huge and dark. 'But I can't say I feel very safe.'

As he spoke, he had the curious sensation that the boat was rocking under him.

'Did you feel that?' whispered Danny, her voice quavering a little.

'I think the sooner we get off the better.' Ned tried to peer over the side and he was shocked to see, through the darkness, what looked like water.

The boat gave another lurch, bigger than before, and suddenly something quite unexpected happened.

'We're floating!' yelled Danny.

The waves had lifted up the boat right off the beach. Next minute, they felt themselves being drawn out to sea. Ned tried to stand up. Perhaps they should jump before it was too late – but when he looked down, he saw it *was* too late. There was water all around.

'We're being taken out to sea!' cried Danny.

'We can't be,' said Ned, 'the tide's coming in.' But perhaps the tide was turning or the wind was stronger than the tide.

Soon there was open sea round them. The boat was no longer buffeted by rollers as they broke, but thrown up and down by waves. They rose and fell so steeply that the boat rode up to the tip of mountains then fell back into deep valleys. Both Ned and Danny were clinging to the rope or they would have been swept off the side.

A new nasty thought struck Ned. Was the boat seaworthy? He'd thought it abandoned, derelict, when he'd played on it in what seemed like another life. He was wondering whether to say anything to Danny, when she spoke herself.

'If this boat sinks, we'll go down with it. We'll drown or die of cold. Even Mab won't be able to save us then.'

Both of them were already extremely chilled. As the clouds broke apart, Ned saw that Danny's face was whiter than a ghost's (certainly than Mab's, he thought sadly) and he guessed his was the same.

'If my hands get any colder,' said Danny in a very small voice, 'I won't be able to hang on.'

'You have to!' answered Ned fiercely.

'I know.'

Ned thought that his tumble in the waves that morning had been nothing compared to what they were going through. Then, it had all been over so quickly he'd hardly felt the cold. Now the cold seemed as bad as being drowned.

'We should sing,' he suggested, but a bigger wave than usual washed away his words.

'What?' asked Danny, when they both surfaced.

'Sing. We should sing.'

'What are you on about!'

'To keep us warm. What songs do you know?'

Danny seemed unconvinced. 'My teeth are chattering

too much to sing and my throat's sore from the seawater.'

'You should keep your mouth shut.'

'How can I keep my mouth shut and sing? You're stupid.'

For some crazy reason, the only song Ned could think of was 'Silent Night, Holy Night', which made him very stupid. Perhaps arguing was as warming as singing.

'Anyway,' added Danny, after they'd been down into one of the deepest valleys and risen up again to the highest mountain, 'In *Titanic*, they sang as the ship went down – and I don't want that to happen.'

'N-No.' Ned's teeth had started to chatter too. He remembered hearing somewhere that chattering teeth kept you warm. Personally, he'd rather have a nice radiator.

'I wish you hadn't brought up that movie.'

'At least we haven't hit an iceberg.'

Rocks! That was a new horror Ned hadn't thought of. If they hit a rock, they'd go down in a flash. But perhaps they were too far out to sea. At least the boat seemed to be bobbing on top of everything the storm flung at her.

'This is a great boat!' he exclaimed.

'A sturdy old fishing boat,' agreed Danny.

Then they both fell silent. The effort to talk at the same time as keeping a grip on the rope was too much.

Five minutes passed. Ned felt a jerk under his hand. Danny had half fallen as one of her hands slipped off the rope.

'Danny!'

'I know. I nearly fell asleep.'

'And let go.'

'I told you, I can't hold on much longer.' She sounded angry.

'I'm going to try and get to the cabin.' Ned had to take action. If he waited they'd both drown. 'I'm sure Dad and Doug will be looking for us now. Once they see the boat's gone, they'll call out the coastguards.'

'They'll send a lifeboat you mean?' Danny's voice had lost its anger but sounded very sleepy. It frightened Ned more than anything.

'There might be an old flare in the cabin. So I can show them where we are.'

'If you leave me, I might not be here when you get back. I'm that cold . . .' Danny's voice slurred and died away.

'Don't be so pathetic!' Ned shrieked.

'Sorry.' He could hardly hear her voice.

'OK. I won't leave you.' He thought there almost certainly wasn't a flare anyway. If only they'd realised what was happening at the beginning, they could have got in the cabin and had a bit of shelter. Now it was too late. Danny was far too weak to get there. Worse still, there was a good half-metre of water in the bottom of the boat. Was it from the waves coming over the side? Or had they sprung a leak?

He looked up at the sky and saw a few stars shining. It had stopped raining and there were fewer clouds. If anyone did come looking for them, they would be easier to spot.

His secret fear was that his dad and Doug wouldn't wake up till the morning. They were both absolutely exhausted. How could he have gone off like that on his own! But then he didn't know all the bad luck that would follow.

'Danny! Danny! You're not to go to sleep!'

'No. No.' But her voice seemed to come from a faraway place.

Then Ned himself must have drifted off.

The next thing he knew was a bright light overhead. He thought vaguely that the moon must have come out to join the stars.

'Danny! Danny!' He reached for her hand. Thankfully, he felt her icy fingers.

'Say something! Danny!' There was no answer.

Overhead, the light became even brighter and a huge rumbling, vibrating sound was even louder than the roar of wind and waves.

28

What happened next? Afterwards Ned could hardly remember, and at the time it was a blur of noise, wind, a man's voice commanding.

He had come from above, a huge figure descending on to the deck. To Ned, dazed and only half conscious, he was more like an angel than a man. But he was real enough. He came down to where they lay and shouted in Ned's ear, 'We'll take the girl first. You're Ned, aren't you? What's her name?'

'Danny,' whispered Ned.

'OK, Danny,' boomed the man, much bigger and stronger in his waterproof overalls than any wave.

'OK, Danny. Can you hear me?'

There was no answer.

'I think she's asleep,' whispered Ned. 'I kept telling her not to.'

'Don't you worry. She'll be fine. I'm going to take her up with me to the helicopter now. You just hang on tight till I'm back.'

This was the first time that Ned took in that it was

a helicopter making the racket above him, and that the bright light was a spotlight shone down on the boat – not the moon.

He'd read about this sort of thing in books and seen it in films, but somehow being involved himself wasn't the same at all. For one thing, everything felt so confused inside his head and outside that he could hardly make out what was going on.

One part of him knew that Danny was being winched up to safety, but the other part only thought about the hard rope under his freezing fingers and how he mustn't let go, he mustn't let go.

Next thing, he felt powerful arms round him and some sort of harness being strapped on his body.

'There's a good lad. You can do it on your own. That's the way.' The man's voice was encouraging in his ear. Then he was swinging in the air, with a perilous sense of space about him, before landing on a hard floor and with more strong arms round him.

'Ned, isn't it? You're all right now, Ned.' He felt himself being wrapped in something hard and bright.

'Danny?' he whispered.

'Don't you worry about Danny. We're taking you both to hospital and they'll look after you there.'

'But is she . . . ?' Ned wanted to say 'alive,' but somehow the word wouldn't get out of his mouth and he found that he'd drifted somewhere warm and faraway.

29

Ned slept all night through. He was in a side room of a children's ward and he woke up to the sound of children's voices.

He opened his eyes slowly. On either side of his bed sat his dad and Doug. His dad was reading a newspaper and Doug was taking a little kip. They both seemed very calm and companionable, as if they didn't have to make conversation like strangers do.

His dad was the first to spot Ned was awake. He put down his paper by his chair and took Ned's hand.

'You know,' he said, 'I was afraid I'd gained one child only to lose another.'

Ned felt too muddled to work out this one. 'I'm sorry.'

'I'm proud of you. You were trying to help your friend.'

'Yes.' Gradually everything was becoming clearer in Ned's head. He took a breath. 'Danny?'

'She's all right. Although not as well as you. Hardly anything wrong with you. You'll be out any time, I shouldn't be surprised. She's skinny, that's the trouble.'

'But you said she's all right. Can I see her?' Ned started to throw off the bedclothes.

'Hey, not so fast. I've promised you she's fine, haven't I?' His voice was firm.

At this, Doug woke up and his old blue eyes fixed on Ned. 'You gave us a fright, young man. The worst night of my life – and that includes bombing raids in the war.'

'Sorry,' mumbled Ned again.

'No apology.' Doug waved his arm. 'Although it does seem a roundabout way to get me to see Danny's baby sister.'

'You've seen her?' Ned pulled himself more upright.

'You've all landed up in the same hospital: you, Ellen, Tony and Danny. Funny the way these things turn out.'

'Hardly funny,' commented Guy.

'Forgive me. I'm old and foolish. Just think, I believed life in England would be peaceful.'

'The thing I want to know when you feel strong enough to tell me,' Guy stood over his son, 'is why you decided to go out to sea in a rotten old tub when a force eight gale was blowing, with spring tides to match.'

'We didn't,' said Ned. 'And don't call it a rotten old tub.' He suddenly felt close to tears. 'That boat saved our lives. It was a *valiant* boat!' He sank back into the bed, trembling, and turned his face to the wall.

'He's quite right.' Doug looked reprovingly at Guy. 'I

know what it's like to be old and undervalued. That boat did a grand job for them.'

'I'm sorry. I'm so sorry. I didn't mean to upset you. You're a bit of a hero, you know that.' Ned's dad tried to see his son's face, with no success.

Ned felt weak and obstinate at the same time. Then he thought that if his dad and Doug hadn't sent help he and Danny might not have survived, so he turned back to face Guy. 'How did you know where we were?'

'The first miracle was that we woke up at all.' Doug leaned forward.

'I was worried about that,' muttered Ned. He didn't really want to re-live his fears on the boat.

'I was out for the count,' continued Doug.

'We both were,' agreed Guy.

'But something woke me up. To be precise,' Doug blinked his rheumy old eyes as if he still couldn't believe it, 'a girl's voice. She went on and on in my ear.'

'Same here,' said Ned's dad. 'Insistent. Same thing over and over and over.'

'What did she say?' asked Ned, who had guessed at once who the voice belonged to.

'She said, "Get up! Ned and Danny need help at sea".'

'Very forceful, she was.' Guy sat down on the bed. '"Ned and Danny need help at sea." She just didn't let up.'

'We met in the hallway: bleary-eyed, both of us; neither of us having a clue who the other was. It would have been comical, if we hadn't been so worried.'

221

'We checked out the bedrooms,' continued Guy, 'and Doug did a bit of explaining, then I rang the police.'

'Neither of us doubted that girl's voice, you see.'

'How odd is that?' asked Ned's dad wonderingly.

'I'll tell you something odder.' Doug looked down at his gnarled hands, almost as if he was embarrassed by what he was going to say. 'If I hadn't known she drowned sixty years ago, I'd have said it was young Mab who was talking in my ear. But then when you get old and deaf you imagine all kinds.

'It *was* Mab,' whispered Ned, lying back in the pillows. 'I might have guessed she wouldn't give up on us.'

But neither of the men heard him because at that moment a talkative nurse carried in a tray with his breakfast. 'Who's got an appetite then? Enough to feed an army!'

'We ticked every box,' smiled Guy. 'We thought you deserved at least six courses: scrambled egg, sausage, bacon, baked beans, cereal, juice . . .'

And somehow Ned found he was astonishingly hungry. Guy and Doug watched approvingly as he wolfed down the six courses in record time.

When he'd finished, Guy stood up again. 'Now I'll see if I can get permission to take you to see Danny.'

It was a very odd sensation to be led by a nurse through the same hospital that he'd explored when looking for Great-Aunt Ellen. Then, he'd been more worried about Doug's odd behaviour than anything.

Now he was dressed in pyjamas, with a terrifying ordeal behind him.

Doug and his dad hadn't been allowed to come because it would be too many people for Danny.

Doug hadn't minded at all. 'I'll be off to see Ellen. She's been in such a state.'

But Guy failed to hide his disappointment at not meeting the mysterious Danny. 'I'll go and have a coffee. Catch up with you later, Ned.' He waved as he went down the corridor.

'You're the hero,' said the nurse chattily, as they turned the corner of yet another corridor. 'It'll be on the news, I wouldn't be surprised.'

Ned stared at her, not quite understanding. She took Ned's arm proprietorially. Ned shook her off. 'I'm fine thanks.'

'You are too,' she said admiringly. 'Out in that storm all night. It's a miracle you survived.'

'It wasn't all night,' said Ned. 'What do you mean about the news?'

'Didn't you know? There've been cameramen, press – from the nationals now, not just the locals. Photographs of the boat before it sank.'

'The boat sank!' Ned looked at her in astonishment.

'Not long after you were winched off. Another ten minutes was all you had left. So they said. Quite put our hospital on the map with all the interest. Maybe we'll get more funding now . . .'

Ned stopped listening as the nurse chatted on. It seemed he and Danny really had escaped by the skin of

223

their teeth. The boat had kept afloat just long enough for the helicopter to lift them off.

'We were lucky,' Ned said, surprising the nurse, who'd moved on to the need for more cleaners in the hospital.

'And you were brave!' She was young, with a pretty face and short curly hair. Ned decided it wasn't such a bad thing to be admired by someone like her. He imagined what his classmates would think if they read about his adventure in the papers. Or even saw him on the TV.

'Here we are!' announced the nurse. They were outside a closed door with a glass panel at the top. 'No more than fifteen minutes and no disturbing talk.'

'No,' promised Ned, although he wasn't sure how he could avoid 'disturbing talk' with Danny. Everything about her life seemed to be disturbing.

The nurse knocked on the door, opened it, and gave Ned a little shove. 'In you go.'

Ned was prepared for a very sick Danny, possibly with tubes attached to her. What he wasn't prepared for was a smiling-faced girl sitting up in bed with a large baby in her arms. Admittedly she did have a tube sticking out from one arm, but that was all.

'Cheers, Ned,' said Danny.

'Hi, Danny,' replied Ned.

'Ma ma ma ma,' sang the baby.

'I'm glad to meet you, Ned,' said a young woman sitting by Danny's bed. She looked rather like the nice nurse: fair curly hair and a pretty face. But Ned could

224

see she was nervous. Her hands twisted all the time in her lap and her eyes were puffy from crying.

'That's my mum,' said Danny quite casually. Then she added, as if proud of the fact, 'She was worried sick.'

'Right. I'm Lyn,' agreed the young woman with an anxious smile.

Ned remembered all the bad things Danny had told him about her mum, then he remembered the monster, Phil. Yet here they were, mother and her daughters, looking really pleased to be in each other's company.

'Ma ma ma ma,' repeated Tony, batting at Danny's face with her little fists.

'Tony's always loved her big sister,' said Lyn. 'She's not been well, you know. In hospital. You'd never guess now.'

'No,' agreed Ned. He wanted to see how Danny was but it was quite difficult with the baby in between. 'You're not too bad, then.'

'No. What was it, Mum, they said I had?'

'Hypothermia. From the cold water. They aren't half surprised you're doing so well.' She looked from Danny to Ned. 'I'll tell you what. I'll take Tony out for a moment. Give you two a chance to talk, whatever.' She gathered up Tony into her arms and Ned thought how young she seemed still. She must have been very very young when she had Danny.

'See you later, Dan.'

Once Lyn had gone, Ned sat down on the empty chair. He found he was feeling a little wobbly.

'Your mum seems OK,' he said tentatively.

Danny looked embarrassed. She put her hand to her face and Ned saw she was blushing, a strange effect with her white skin and the remains of her multicoloured bruising. 'I know what you're thinking. You're thinking, what was I on about and all. Her not liking me. But the thing is – oh I dunno – Tony being ill, me running away and then nearly dying. She says she knows what's important to her now.'

'But what about Phil?'

'She'd turned him out already. He told us that. Now he's been picked up by the police.'

'I see.' Ned thought about it. 'I told you, didn't I, my dad's back?'

'Well, he was always going to, wasn't he? What about your mum? And the baby?'

'They're coming in a few days.'

'That's nice.' Danny looked at Ned and Ned looked at Danny.

'We'll stay friends, won't we?' said Ned. 'You could visit Lilac Cottage.'

'When Doug and his bride are settled in, you mean. Finished their honeymoon.' They both smiled at the thought of this and how it all came about. 'That old fellow did nab me,' added Danny.

'He sure did. Even if he only wanted to ask you some questions.'

'And you sprang me.' There was a pause. They were both becoming awkward about all this looking back. But Danny still had something to say. 'And you saved my life. Telling me to hang on to that bit of rope. Keeping me awake.'

'Mab saved you. She stopped you walking into the sea. Then she woke up my dad and Doug. Talked into their ears. Told them we needed help at sea. They didn't know who or what it was.'

'But they got up?'

'A miracle, that's what Doug called it. So I didn't tell him about Mab. Well, I did, but he didn't hear. I thought he was going to guess but he never did.'

There was another pause. Ned saw that Danny was looking tired. He'd stayed over the nurse's fifteen minutes and everything they'd talked about was disturbing.

'I don't expect we'll see Mab again,' said Danny, her voice low. 'We're on our own now.'

'Not exactly on our own.' Ned began to shift on his chair. He could see that Danny's eyes were beginning to close. It was time he was off. So when the pretty nurse reappeared, he allowed himself to be led away. Just one backward glance to see she was asleep and then out into the corridor, where Lyn was approaching with Tony in her arms and the nurse beside her.

'She's asleep,' Ned said.

Lyn laid her hand on his pyjama sleeve. 'It was you who rang me, wasn't it?'

'Yes. I . . .'

'I was that low.'

'I'm sorry,' said Ned, although he didn't really feel it.

'Don't you say that. It's me who's sorry. That's

enough now.' She was trying to smile but Ned could see she was nearer tears. All this emotion was a bit much. Ned ducked his head and looked away. 'Thanks due to you. That's it. Now then, nurse, take him away before I go silly on you.'

'He's a hero, that's what he is!' announced the nurse.

This was too much for Ned. He was off down the corridor, leaving the two women behind. He just heard Lyn's voice confiding, 'And he saw off my Phil too,' before he turned the corner. Now life could become ordinary again.

30

In one way life did become ordinary again. There was no Mab – as Danny had predicted – no bearded tramp, no hiding, no terrifying tussles with the sea.

On the other hand, it was quite an event when Ned's mum arrived with the new baby on the very same day that Aunt Ellen was wheeled out from hospital triumphantly by Doug. 'Our legs may be a bit shaky but our hearts are strong!' as he'd announced.

Since Lilac Cottage couldn't fit so many, Ned and his family took two rooms above the Admiral's Poop pub in Seaburgh.

It was strange to be living in such a close family way; even stranger to have the tiny baby, who seemed to either sleep or scream. But Ned noticed that his parents were paying him much more attention than usual. They made a point of asking what he would like to do at the start of each day. It was as if they understood that what had happened and what he'd had to do over the last week had given him the right to a new kind of independence.

Nor did they make the mistake of asking too many questions. They were just there, warm and comfortable.

The day after Ned came out of hospital, the papers were full of the story of two children's narrow escape from drowning. There were even several reporters and cameramen outside Lilac Cottage.

But Ned didn't want to talk about it and his dad made sure he was protected from them.

'That's what dads are for,' he told Ned, 'to protect their children.' And Ned smiled nicely, although he couldn't help thinking his dad hadn't done a brilliant job about that up to now.

It seemed even that was going to change. Ned's mum explained one evening when his dad had gone to London and they were having fish and chips, that they would be cutting down on their foreign travel.

'Dad's got an idea for a book based in England,' she said. 'So we won't be away anything like so much.'

Ned couldn't help guessing that this had more to do with the new baby than him – she was now called Daisy – but it was still good news, if it actually turned out that way. No more lonely holidays at school or with cousins he didn't like. His mum even suggested taking him out of boarding school, once they had settled, and finding a local day school.

'That'd be great!' he encouraged her. There was one place he would still want to visit. 'I'll be able to get to Lilac Cottage, won't I?'

'Of course, darling.' The 'darling' had a cosy sound,

even though Daisy was taking up most of his mum's attention. 'Ellen and Doug have already invited you for as much of the summer holidays as you want. You and Danny too. They plan to pitch a tent in the garden. They say the place is filled with children then and the sea is calm enough to swim.'

Ned's mum looked up just in time to catch the expression on her son's face. 'You don't *have* to swim.'

'No,' he said, 'I don't *have* to do anything. But I expect I will!'

FAR OUT!

Rachel Billington

Ruby is used to being thought stupid and cowardly, but she did see the weird card on the school notice board, with its swirly colours and irresistible invitation: AUDITION FOR LIFE, RING . . .

Strangely, only one other person saw it – cool, streetwise Slate, who wouldn't normally be seen dead talking to kids like Ruby. SO begins an unlikely partnership and an even odder journey . . . across the sea to an island beyond their wildest imaginings.